Seven For The Slab

Seven For The Slab

– *a horror portmanteau* –

Doug Lamoreux

Copyright (C) 2016 Doug Lamoreux
Layout design and Copyright (C) 2016 Creativia
Published 2016 by Creativia
Cover art by http://www.thecovercollection.com/
Edited by Silvia Curry
This book is a work of fiction. Names, characters, places, and incidents are the product of the author's imagination or are used fictitiously. Any resemblance to actual events, locales, or persons, living or dead, is purely coincidental.
All rights reserved. No part of this book may be reproduced or transmitted in any form or by any means, electronic or mechanical, including photocopying, recording, or by any information storage and retrieval system, without the author's permission.

Author's Note

Seven for the Slab (a horror portmanteau) is my first novella, a short novel, written in honor of my movie-going, terror-filled childhood, and particularly in remembrance of the works of Amicus Films, the fright-filled British 'anthology' movies upon which I grew up; Tales From the Crypt, Vault of Horror, The House That Dripped Blood, Dr. Terror's House of Horrors, From Beyond the Grave, and on and on. Seven for the Slab is my ode to those wondrous days. It is a compilation of short stories (three previously published, four written specifically for inclusion here) stirred together into one tale. Don't take it too seriously. Have fun.

Doug Lamoreux, August 2016

The Procedure – copyright 2013 by Doug Lamoreux The HORROR SOCIETY'S 2013 IGOR AWARD winner. Originally published in The Best of the Horror Society 2013 by The Horror Society.
D is for Dead – and Disappointment – copyright 2013 by Doug Lamoreux Originally published on-line in the '2013 Halloween Emotional Outbreak Marathon' by the Books From Hale blog site.
Appetites – copyright 2011 by Doug Lamoreux Originally published on-line by Short n' Scary Stories.

The Chameleon – copyright 2016 by Doug Lamoreux
The Rookie – copyright 2016 by Doug Lamoreux
A Little Respect – copyright 2016 by Doug Lamoreux
It's a Living – copyright 2016 by Doug Lamoreux
Seven for the Slab – copyright 2016 by Doug Lamoreux

Acknowledgments

This book would not exist had not Milton Subotsky and Max J. Rosenberg created, and Robert Bloch written for, Amicus Films. Amicus would not have been without Hammer Films. And, whatever I am, I would not have been without either. And, Jenny, of course. There are no books without Jenny.

*Dedicated to
Elton D. Graff
For what seemed a thousand dark movies in a
hundred dark theaters;
for teen years that cannot be repeated and will not be
forgotten.*

One

There are few things as startling and, thereafter, as unsettling as a ringing telephone in the dead of night.

It repeatedly stabs the air, then the ear, then the psyche, driving deeper and deeper, until finally it reaches and awakens the conscious mind. It pulls the innocent from the blissful peace of sleep into a dark cold world of reality in which someone wants something from them, or needs to deliver life-altering news to them, or is compelled to level a shock from which they might never recover. Even if the call rescues them from the throes of a fitful sleep, or the bizarre terrors of a nightmare, it hardly feels the rescuer. For, until it is picked up, the ringing phone is a harbinger of the unknown.

What is more frightening than the unknown? How many phone calls bring good news in the middle of the night?

To even consider those questions makes it difficult to understand Herb Flay's glee, his absolute delight, at being roused from sleep by his ringing phone. But once he was awake, sitting up in bed and could identify the incessant noise, once he'd scooped up the receiver and managed a gravelly, "Hello," once he'd heard and recognized the voice on the other end and gathered the incoming message, he was delighted indeed.

It was the call he'd been waiting for, waiting and waiting. It was the call he'd given up hope of ever receiving. Now it had come. It mattered not a whit that it was one o'clock in the morning. It mattered even less there was at that moment a torrential downpour taking place outside, a fierce thunderstorm into which that call would force him to venture. Nothing mattered now. The call had come. He was relieved beyond words. He was happy as a lark.

Two people had been found dead!

Herb Flay worked for a funeral home, the Fengriffen Funeral Home and Crematorium to be precise. It was a revelation that frequently caused queasy twists in the listeners' stomachs or the feeling of cold fingers climbing their spines, but it needn't have. Flay was used to the reactions, the discomfited pauses, the wary looks, the interesting and alarmed noises people made, involuntarily or on purpose, when they learned he worked at a funeral home; that he worked with the dead. "Hey," Flay would tell them with a smile, "it's a living."

For the record, Herb Flay – and his boss, Mortician Marlowe Blake, and their Fengriffen Funeral Home – resided in the mid-sized Illinois town of Sturm's Landing (population 32,000). It was named after its founder, Mark Von Sturm, a ferry operator on a mighty river that, in the century and a half that followed, had shrunk to a trickling creek. Over those same decades, the local economy did likewise. So had the funeral business. It all seemed to drain away. But it wasn't finished, not yet, not that night.

The remains of what once were two human beings lay in a house in the sleepy village of Cedartown, thirteen miles away, awaiting removal. There was much to do. Flay scrambled for his clothes.

He wasn't the only one.

The bodies had been discovered by Sheriff's Deputies Christopher Maitland and Philip Grayson nearly two hours earlier, well before the Witching Hour. The Sheriff's Department had been alerted by a neighbor who reported, "Something (at the house on the end of their block) seems amiss." Maitland and Grayson responded, in separate squad cars, from separate ends of the county; Maitland arriving twenty minutes ahead of his brother officer. Unable to get a response from anyone inside, Maitland was suspicious of trouble and, more to the point, alarmed by the condition of the house. When Grayson arrived, Maitland shared his concerns. The deputies notified their dispatcher, who roused the sheriff and called an ambulance and the Cedartown Volunteer Fire Department.

A Fire Department engine and ladder truck, and an ambulance from the Sturm's Landing Rural service, arrived on the scene at a small split level with a mock colonial front porch built on a hill over top of its own garage in a quiet residential section of the village. The sheriff would begrudgingly be on his way, the officers imagined, though neither had heard from him personally. They decided not to wait for their superior. With the aid of the ladder truck driver, and a weighted bar from one of the truck's compartments, the lock on the front door of the house was gingerly knocked in.

The door flew open. The decayed breath of Satan, a rotting stench from the deepest pits of Hell, escaped past them out the door.

With the ambulance crew waiting anxiously by the door, holding their collective breath against the stink, the deputies entered the house by themselves. They did a quick search up and down, found what they found and, without disturbing anything further, made a hasty retreat. Back outside, they gulped air to keep from vomiting and told the ambulance and fire personnel the acute nature of the emergency was past... long past. When he could breathe again through his mouth, Maitland took up his portable radio and asked their dispatcher to notify the coroner that his services were required. That was as far as things had progressed.

Without going into details unnecessary for the present, suffice to say that the two corpses the county deputies discovered inside were... in bad shape. The pair, as yet unidentified, had evidently 'passed on' some considerable time before. They looked it. They certainly smelled it. And, now that the seal had been broken on the front door, the entire neighborhood was quickly taking on the same odor; the air stunk to high heaven of rotting human flesh.

Standard Operating Procedures for a fire or crime scene with multiple responding emergency services required the establishment of a Command Post. Mind you, nothing was on fire and nobody was certain a crime had been committed. But, with more than one body and no immediate hint as to cause of death, a few assumptions had to be made until facts could be gathered. Therefore, until further notice, a crime was assumed and a Command Post established. In the big city, they'd roll in a flashy trailer for that purpose with a police or fire logo splashed across its side. But this wasn't New York City or Los Angeles, this was the village of Cedartown, Illinois (population 900). The Command Post and, owing to the rain coming down in buckets, the rest and drying off area, on this occasion would be a neighbor's garage across the street and a half-block away. It was near enough they could quickly be on scene to do their jobs but far enough away that, though they couldn't escape the stench, the distance and the storm might lessen its gut-churning effects.

The garage space was suggested and donated by the same curious neighbor who'd spotted something amiss and called the police in the first place, a fat, over-talkative fellow in his late forties with still dark but thinning hair in a comb-over, a handle-bar mustache, and wire glasses with double thick lenses. He'd be pleased and proud, he said, if they'd use his garage for their meeting place and ran ahead to make the coffee. Despite the fact not one of the cops, firemen, or ambulance crew liked him much, nobody objected to his offer. It was raining like hell.

That's how the lion's share of the police officers, firefighters, and paramedics responding to the scene came to be gathered in the nosy neighbor's garage, drying off, looking forward to hot coffee, and awaiting word and a call to action from their superiors. They included: Deputy Chris Maitland of the Dortmun County Sheriff's Department; a brand spanking new paramedic, Lisa Clayton, from Sturm's Landing Rural; and representing the Cedartown Fire Department, veteran Firefighter John Reid and a still wet-behind-the-ears recruit, Ward Baker.

Their host could be seen gallivanting about, through what must have been his kitchen window, in an unattached house sixty feet or so from the garage. He'd left the garage's overhead door invitingly open for their arrival, a space by his lawn tools cleared away from whatever coats and gear they wanted to hang or dispense with, and a table, quickly constructed out of sawhorses and two-by-fours, with napkins, paper plates, and a tower of hot/cold drinking cups already in place.

By unanimous agreement of the gathered civil servants, the overhead door was ratcheted closed again in hopes of deadening the offensive smell just that little bit more. The thunderstorm, though, would not be denied. It continued to boom outside and flash brilliantly through the row of garage door windows.

The garage owner danced in from the darkness through the walk-in door, with a humungous serving tray (covered against the rain) in his hands. He pulled off his yellow rain slicker, rolled up his shirt sleeves, and began happily serving coffee to the wet emergency workers. Despite the rank odor in the air, he was beaming as if he'd won the lottery and clearly having the time of his life. No sooner did he get their cups full then he was back in his slicker and headed out again in search of more goodies.

He passed Maitland's partner, Deputy Grayson, coming in. Grayson closed the door behind him against the storm. The deputy's brown uniform shirt and tan pants were protected and dry but his gray plastic rain smock was drenched. He shook like a dog shedding water. The gathered gave Grayson their attention, while Maitland voiced their communal question, "Anything new?"

"No." Grayson shook his shower cap-covered trooper's hat as the floor beneath became a modern art masterpiece of water splashed on concrete. "I left the ladder truck driver... I'm sorry, I'm terrible with names."

"Henderson," Baker, the younger of the two firefighters, put in. "Paul Henderson."

Grayson nodded. "I left Henderson and... the engine driver?"

"Sandy Lund," Reid, the other firefighter, said.

"Lund," Grayson agreed, then added, "Boy, has she got a mouth on her?"

"Yes," both firefighters said in unison. "She does."

Grayson hung his slicker on the wall, with the others, and his hat over that. Turning back, he spotted the EMT, Clayton, a little blonde in a blue uniform, and was reminded, "Oh, and the other paramedic." He held the look. "Your boss?"

Lisa didn't snort but looked as if she wanted to. "My partner," she said, correcting him, then changed it again to reluctantly split the difference. "My lead, Abner Perry."

Grayson nodded. "Like I said, I'm terrible with names. I left those three babysitting the rigs outside the house, watching the front door, and keeping an eye for a crowd."

"You're expecting one?" Clayton asked.

"A crowd? Usually, yes. Make that 'always'... a crowd. But with the storm – and the stink – no one has braved it yet."

"Except our host," Maitland said, jutting a thumb at the wall and, by implication, at the fellow's house beyond. "The guy you just met in the doorway. The neighbor who found the bodies and phoned it in. He's getting more coffee, bless his heart."

"What's his name?"

Maitland considered the question, then shrugged. "Heck, I don't remember. I'm not much better with names than you are. Schreck, I think, or Shock, or Shanks... it's in my notes. I've just been thinking of him as 'the Proprietor'."

Grayson chuckled. "That's because you like big words."

"What about our fire chief," Baker asked, interrupting. "Wasn't he out there?"

"The old war horse? Yes," Grayson said. "He's at the scene; sitting in the engine. He goes without saying. They're waiting on the sheriff and the coroner, just like us. Nothing to do but wait."

Baker sighed. He stared out one of the windows, down the block in the direction of the house, though the darkness and the rain prevented him seeing anything beyond the diffused red, blue, and yellow flickers of the emergency vehicles' lights. "Geez," he said. "I feel like I should be out there. But I just... Just the smell alone... I don't know how they can handle it. Three minutes and my guts were doing cartwheels."

Grayson nodded understanding, then turned to Clayton again. "Your lead was looking a might green around the gills," he told her. "He's sitting in your ambulance now, holding a cracked ammonia capsule, and taking hits off of it. He's *not* having a good time. But the other three... They've been on the Fire Department a long time."

Reid laughed. "I'm sure they've all smelled death before."

"It's more than death," the young firefighter went on, "it's a horror show." As if to highlight Baker's comment, thunder cracked outside and lightning flashed through the windows.

"You haven't seen it up close," Maitland said. "It is a perfect night for horror, no doubt. For ghosts and ghouls, for murder and mayhem, for tales of things that go bump in the stormy night."

Clayton blew a raspberry and returned to sipping her coffee.

"Aw, come on, Lisa." Until then, Reid had kept his heavy turnout coat on. Now he peeled it off, hung it in the corner to dry, and stood in a blue T-shirt (a firefighters' Maltese Cross emblazoned on his left breast), yellow bunker pants, and boots, with his thumbs hitched under his red suspenders like a farmer in his field. "What's the matter? You don't like war stories? It's tradition," Reid went on, "whenever cops, firefighters, and EMTS get together, they tell stories. At times like this, they're a professional requirement."

Reid paused for the chuckles of agreement.

"Now they're out of bed, our bosses, the sheriff and the coroner, when they get here, will take their sweet time assessing the scene, screwing the pooch, and feeling important. When they've had enough, unless these gentlemen. . . " Reid pointed at the county deputies for emphasis. ". . . didn't see what they saw, we'll have to wait for the funeral parlor to come scoop up whatever is left."

Coming out of his momentary funk, Baker laughed and nodded at Clayton. "He's right, Lisa. We've got plenty of time to kill. You better tell us a war story."

"I'm a new paramedic," she exclaimed, "as new as you are. I don't have any war stories yet."

More laughter followed, this time from all. Then a particularly impressive arc of lightning flashed and a roll of thunder drowned them out. The garage went quiet and all that could be heard was the drumming of rain on the roof. More than one in the group lifted their cups close to their faces. Their suddenly rapid breathing made fog on the surface of their coffee and stirred the odor of fresh brew to dull the smell of death in the air.

"Okay, the paramedic needs to think about it for a minute," Maitland called out. "Someone else then. A war story. But, in honor of the creepy night and situation, make it a horror story."

The deputy scanned the group but there seemed to be no takers.

"How about you?" Grayson asked. "You're never short a story, partner. Start us off."

"I can if I have to," Maitland said. "We've had plenty of experiences."

The walk-in door burst open. The Proprietor stumbled in, kicked the door closed, and fell against it as if holding back the storm with his ample body. He blindly pulled a fresh pot of coffee and two boxes of cookies from beneath his coat. Blindly, as his thick glasses were fogged and his face a waterfall from comb-over to glasses, to mustache, to chin. With his hands full, he could do nothing about either.

Clayton took the coffee pot. Baker relieved him of the cookies, bleating, "Hey! How appropriate is that?" He waved the boxes. "Devil's Food!"

The emergency workers chuckled their appreciation. The poor Proprietor, swiping at his watery mug with his now free hands, didn't get the joke and innocently looked his confusion.

"Don't worry about it," Grayson told him. "He likes your choice of snacks."

"Oh!" their host said, with no further evidence the light of understanding had been lit.

"Deputy Maitland was about to tell us a war story," Clayton said. "And a horror story?"

The deputy smiled. "I think it fills both requirements. But perhaps our host would rather..."

"Oh," the Proprietor said with something between alarm and delight, "don't stop on my account. I'd love to hear one."

"You've got me curious," Grayson said. "And we've got time. Go ahead, partner, tell it."

"Yeah," Baker agreed with enthusiasm. "Tell it."

"All right," Maitland said, accepting a hot refill to his cup. "I will." He declined a cookie, fortified himself with a careful sip of coffee, and looked to the garage rafters above their heads as if searching for a way to begin. He found it, took on a serious expression and, quite out of nowhere, said, "The restaurant was nice."

Two

No, the restaurant was better than nice. It was beautiful. Wood this, leather that, lit crystal above, silver and honest-to-god china all around on table coverings looking better than her bed linens. Imagine, a tablecloth you'd want to sleep on. The her? She was Vicki Robbins. She had come, on purpose, without an invitation yet it was just then dawning on her that she didn't belong in that fancy restaurant. It showed. Her red-lipsticked mouth hung open.

"Good evening, *Madame*," the la-de-da guy at the reservation podium said. "May I help you?"

He looked like a waiter only more important. Vicki knew he was the mate-er-dee (though she wasn't sure of the pronunciation and couldn't spell it). "Oh, I don't know," she said, stumbling out of the gate. "I think so, maybe. *Eh*, can you tell me, is there a Mr. Canning here?"

"*Monsieur* Canning?" the maître d' repeated. His eyebrow jumped but fell back into place so quickly Vicki hardly noticed it. "Certainly, *Madame*," he continued. "He is expecting you."

"Well, I'm not sure that he is." Vicki's smile quavered. "Actually, I'm sure that he isn't." She was off to the races. "He might be. Well, not expecting me, I don't mean that. He's expecting somebody else. But he might be glad I came. Maybe."

The maître d' stared, this time without reacting at all. He wasn't paid to react. Instead, he snapped his fingers, pointed at a near-twin who slid silently behind the podium in his place and, smiling pleasantly at the young woman, passed his hand toward the dining room. "Please, follow me."

They passed a guy in a monkey suit playing a piano. It was nice but nothing to line dance to. Then Vicki saw him, for the second time that day, just beyond the *maître d's* arm. He was a good-looking man with bad-looking hair, dark and very like the business end of a bottle brush – but with kind eyes, an expensive blue suit, and shoes without scuffs featuring neither a brand name nor a swish, seated by himself at a table set for two. Yeah, it was Mr. Canning, all right. He looked up as they arrived, smiling, but with questions in his eyes. The *maître d'* reached for the chair opposite. "*Madame.*"

"S'cuse me," Vicki said, laying her hand on his lapel. "I better not sit yet. I don't know if he'll want me to." She turned to the man at the table. "Mr. Canning, you don't know me." Vicki hurried her speech on before he had her chased out. "You might recognize me, 'cause you saw me at your doctor's office this morning. I'm Vicki Robbins. I, *eh*, file medical records for the doctor, the doctor you saw today, Dr. Lundgren. I was there when you left. Really, I was there when you came in too, which I guess is more important, 'cause that's when you asked the receptionist, Donna Rogers, little blonde, split-ends, if she'd have dinner with you tonight. And she said yes, then you asked

13

her to meet you here at The Vineyard." Vicki turned to tell the *maître d'*, "You have a beautiful restaurant, by the way," because when you're making a fool of yourself, you need all the friends you can get.

"*Merci*. Thank you, *Madame*."

"You're welcome, I'm sure." She returned to Mr. Canning as if she'd never left. "But then, after you left, Donna realized she couldn't make it. So, well, here I am. I mean, I'm Vicki and, if you want me... I mean, if you wouldn't mind my taking her place, I'd love to have dinner with you—instead." She caught her breath, then added, "Donna chews with her mouth open."

There. She was done. Real silverware *tinked*, actual crystal glasses *clinked*, elegant noises surrounded them in their awkward moment. Vicki might have blushed pink with embarrassment, but she wasn't the type. Mr. Canning, on the other hand, blushed ever so slightly. Then he pushed his chair back and stood. "Please, *eh*..."

"Vicki."

He smiled. The smile, like the restaurant, was nice. "Vicki, of course. Please. Join me." Then he told the *maître d'*, "A bottle of champagne. Something nice."

"*Oui, Monsieur*."

"Oh, champagne!" Vicki sighed, scooching her chair in. "This is so nice. I don't remember the last time I ate out where the waiter didn't have a cardboard hat and ask if I wanted the meal or just the sandwich." She giggled nervously and, when Mr. Canning laughed too, went on. "When you signed in at the clinic, when you asked Donna out tonight, I admit, I was a little jealous. 'Cause, I mean, you're good looking, and a nice dresser, and you told her

The Vineyard which means you have money. Not that that matters, but of course it does, a little. Then after, when you came out of the exam room, and you told the doctor..."

"You heard that?"

"Well, I was right there. I couldn't help but hear. I wasn't trying to eavesdrop, I swear, but I couldn't help but hear. I'm sorry if I've embarrassed you."

"I'm not embarrassed, Miss... Robbins?"

"Vicki, please."

"Vicki. I'm not embarrassed, either by my condition or my attempts at remedy. And I never meant to imply you'd eavesdropped. What I said was no secret. I merely told your Dr. Lundgren that there was nothing more to be said."

"You sure did," Vicki exclaimed.

It had been a little bit of a scene. Mr. Canning had come from the office exam room in a huff with the surgeon, Dr. Lundgren, talking to his back. Then, sure enough, Mr. Canning had told him, not angrily, but certainly forcefully, "There's nothing more to be said. If you won't do it, you won't!"

The doctor, apparently still trying to explain his position on whatever it was they had discussed, told him, "Mr. Canning, please. Even if I agreed with your understanding of your condition, the procedure you want is... Well, I'm sorry, but it's simply out of the question. If we could take this back into the exam room..."

"No," Mr. Canning had said. "There's seems little point in that."

The little bit of a scene was memorable mostly because after Mr. Canning thanked the doctor for his time, he apologized to Donna, and Vicki thought

15

maybe her too, because he said, "Forgive me, ladies. I didn't mean to make a scene." Then he asked Donna if they were still on for dinner. She replied that they were, and Mr. Canning left.

Vicki smiled at Mr. Canning across the fancy dinner table. "Then Donna changed her mind," she said. "So here I am."

He nodded slowly. "Did Donna say why she changed her mind?"

"Oh, I was afraid of that," Vicki said. She bit her bottom lip. "I guess I'm not your type, huh?"

"No, it isn't that. Donna's not really my type, either. I was just curious."

Vicki didn't want to tell him what had happened next. It had been another scene in itself. She didn't want to say, not knowing how he'd take it, but Dr. Lundgren's nurse had stuck her nose in. No sooner had Mr. Canning left then she, the nurse that is, came right up to Donna's desk and asked, "You're not going out with that guy, are you?" When Donna nodded, she said, "You might want to reconsider."

Vicki's co-worker asked why, of course, and the nurse said, "Well, I can't say; he *is* a patient. I mean he's not contagious but... Let's just say, he's a lulu of a patient. Do yourself a big favor, sweetie, find something else to do tonight."

Donna made up her mind, then and there, she wasn't going. Then she decided she wasn't going to let Mr. Canning know, either. That didn't seem right to Vicki. Not right at all. Besides she, Vicki that is, hadn't been out in a long time. So she took a chance herself and here she was. Now Mr. Canning wanted to know why; of course, he did. She didn't really want to tell him, not all of it, not about Donna. She wouldn't be there except for Donna. She sort of owed her not to tell on her. And she didn't want to hurt Mr. Canning's feelings, not before they ordered. So, it seemed, making an excuse for Donna was the best approach. "She couldn't make it. Her mama's sick," Vicki told him. "So I intruded."

"It's no intrusion, Miss Robbins."

"Vicki."

"Vicki. I'm glad you came. Sitting alone would have been embarrassing. Some might say I've already embarrassed myself enough for one day."

"But you didn't at all. Don't think that. I'm sorry Dr. Lundgren couldn't help you."

"I didn't actually think he would." He shrugged. "I took a chance."

"See, we have something in common. We both take chances." They shared a smile. "Do you mind, Mr. Canning—"

"Lancelot. That's my, *eh*, first name."

"Lancelot? Really? Like the knight in shining armor?"

He blushed redder still. "My friends call me, Lance. Call me Lance, Vicki."

"All right, Lance. Do you mind, Lance, if I ask... just what your medical condition is?"

"Don't you know?" Lance seemed amazed. "I assumed the whole office had a laugh at my expense after I left."

"Oh, no! We're not that way. I'm certainly not that way."

"No. Your presence here proves that. It's just that few understand the condition I have. Most find the whole idea repulsive. And they certainly wouldn't discuss it over dinner."

"I work in a doctor's office. I've seen and heard it all. What procedure did you want done?"

"I wanted the doctor to amputate my left arm."

"My God! What's wrong with your arm?"

"As far as I know, not a thing."

Later, much later, a key turned in the lock and the door to Lancelot Canning's apartment swung inward. Backlit by the hallway light, Lance and Vicki, their arms full, both teetering drunk, stumbled through laughing. The darkness swallowed them as Lance pushed the door shut again.

"I can't do this!" Vicki said in a slurred whisper. "This is crazy. I should just go home. I've had too much to drink and this is crazy."

"No, no! You promised."

"But you can't hold me to that," Vicki insisted. "This is crazy!"

"Okay, wait. Wait. Wait." Lance found the switch, the lights blinked on, and they blinked too. "At least have a nightcap with me. We'll talk about it."

"O-kay, one nighty-nightcap." Her arms were full, a paper bag in one, a long, thin package in the other. "Oh, I'm so wasted. I can barely talk and I can't keep my eyes open. They must have thought we were nuts in that store. Where... whew... where do you want this stuff?"

"Anywhere," Lance told her. "The desk, a chair. I'm gonna stick the ice in the freezer." On the way out, he turned back to see Vicki laying her burdens on the couch. "Oh, not there! That might ruin the cushion." He pointed to a breakfast nook against the wall. "Put the saw on the table."

Vicki shrugged. It was no skin off her nose. Then she thought maybe she shouldn't think like that and laughed quietly. Too much alcohol. The table was farther away than it had looked and the room was shifting, which didn't help, but she made it across and set down the sack and hacksaw as instructed. She slid her jacket off too and took no notice when it missed the table completely and dropped to the floor. "God, this is insane," she whispered. "Oh, my head is swimming. I better sit down."

The return to the couch was strangely farther than the trip to the table had been, and she sank over the arm and onto the end cushion with relief. Safely off her feet, Vicki called out, "What's it called?"

Lance stepped from the kitchen drying a massive butcher's knife. "What's what called?"

Vicki made one of those *tsk-tsk* noises of impatience. Hadn't they only just been discussing it? "Your arm thing. The condition. What's your condition called?"

"I told you in the cab." He tossed the towel back into the kitchen and laid the knife on the table beside the still-packaged hacksaw. "It's called BID. Body Integrity Identity Disorder. Some call it Body Dysmorphia. Some just call it nuts. It's a rare condition that is characterized..." He took a breath; he'd been drinking too. "Characterized by an overwhelming desire... to amputate one or more of your own limbs. What are you drinking?"

"It doesn't make any sense." She heard the *clink* of ice and realized he'd moved again. It took a moment to find him, over by the little wet-bar thingy, doing – something.

"What," he asked with a big grin, "is nonsensical about drinking?"

"Huh?" Drinks! So that's what he was doing. "No! Drinking makes sense. I'll take gin, if you have it. If you haven't, I'll take anything. Cutting off a perfectly good arm, *that* doesn't make any sense."

"That's what makes it a disorder." He poured the drinks and headed her way. "Of course, *I* don't see it that way. To me, it doesn't belong; the arm, I mean. It's not mine. It's wrong, and I want it gone."

Vicki took her drink and sipped. "I don't understand."

"You're not alone. Few do. The desire, the need, to be disabled seems so bizarre and contrary to what most people think is normal. Those of us who suffer a dysmorphia, we keep it to ourselves."

"We?"

"I'm not alone. Believe me, there are others. Who knows how many. You saw Lundgren's reaction. You should have heard him before we left the exam room. He said. . . " Lance cleared his throat and did a pretty good impersonation of the doctor's voice. At least it sounded good to Vicki's dulled sense of hearing. " 'You're on a slippery slope, Mr. Canning.' That's what he said. Then he said, 'I have no intention of joining you. I won't push the envelope for an impaired person who isn't in touch with reality, and I can't dignify your *idea* of normalcy by mangling your healthy body'." Lance washed the speech down with his whiskey.

"You can't blame him."

"The hell I can't. It's judgmental attitudes like that, and a complete lack of medical options, that force BID sufferers to treat themselves. Forces them to take extreme measures to paralyze or amputate themselves... like we're going to do." Lance turned and focused on her. "Vicki," he asked with feeling, "you *are* still with me?"

"I don't know," Vicki said, then yawned wide and long. "I'm sorry. The alcohol. You made me drunk. I'm so tired. You were... saying... people with this... problem... have done this before?"

Nodding, Lance dropped onto the couch beside her. "I read of one guy who froze his leg off with dry ice. Another blew one off with a shotgun. I knew a man who paid ten thousand dollars for an illegal amputation in Mexico, then died of gangrene. And I have firsthand experience. I see the shock on your face. Yes, I've tried to cut my arm off. More than once. I put it under a truck to crush it. The jack collapsed the wrong direction and I walked away with two arms and a black eye."

"Oh, you poor thing."

"I didn't give up," Lance said. "How could I? My left arm doesn't belong to me and my brain won't let me forget it. I tried to saw it off with a table saw. I practiced on animals."

"Oh, how could you?"

"No. I didn't hurt any! I mean, I practiced on animal parts that I got from a butcher. I practiced taking them apart at the joints. I got good at it but, when it came to the saw, I lost my nerve."

Vicki stared, trying to focus. "I don't think it's losing your nerve to *not* cut your own arm off."

"That's exactly what it was. And it's not my arm! For days I drove around, countless hours, endless miles, just driving with that arm dangling out the window, hoping, praying someone would sideswipe the car and rip the arm off. Geez, Vicki, am I boring you? You're fading, your eyes are slits."

She fought through another yawn. "I'm sorry. Please, go on."

"Not much more to tell. Psychiatry doesn't work. Medication doesn't work. Surgery is the only cure and too many people are forced to take matters into their own hands... like us."

"Why us? Aren't there... any doctors... who can help?"

"There was a surgeon in Scotland. He amputated a few legs; gave several men their freedom. But they've made him stop. It's ridiculous. This isn't new. Over two hundred years ago, in France, a guy held a gun to a surgeon's head and forced him to amputate his leg. After, he sent a 'thank you' note saying the doctor had made him 'the happiest of all men.'"

She was yawning again. "Happy?"

"No one enjoys this dysfunction. We don't know how we got it. It's mental torture. It's worse than phantom limb syndrome, where amputees feel pain in lost limbs. Some neurologists think they found a dysfunction in the right parietal lobe that interrupts the body's map of a unified self."

"Huh?"

"The senses don't coalesce. I feel my arm. But it feels wrong... added on."

Vicki was fighting now, yawning between every few words. "And you really want us to... I'd do anything to relieve your suffering, Lance. But I don't know how to cut your arm off!"

"I'll guide you," he told her, then added, "while I'm conscious. Vicki, I'm determined. You promised you'd help." He pointed to the sack on the table. "We bought tourniquets and bandages for the bleeding, a fresh cell phone in case... things get out of hand. We're ready. You're ready. You're so compassionate. You *do* understand. You're just like Davina."

"I just... to tell the truth, I'm a little dizzy. I don't... what's the matter with me? I'm suddenly so... I don't know. I'm sorry. You were..." She stopped. She turned her eyes hard on him. "Who's Davina? Oh, hell, you have a girlfriend."

"No, I don't. Don't worry; no. Not anymore. I mean, Davina *was* my girlfriend. Davina is dead. Dead and gone almost a year. She was like you, Vicki, understanding. She understood that living a lie is the worst human punishment."

"Oh," Vicki said, understanding (and yawning) again. "You poor, poor... I feel so bad for you. And, you know something, Lancelot, you're not a weirdo."

"*Eh*, thanks."

"I have a confession, Lance. I lied to you." Out of nowhere, Vicki got emotional. "I lied to protect your feelings. There's nothing wrong with Donna's mama. The rude bitch said she dodged a bullet and agreed with Lundgren's nurse you were a weirdo. She ditched you. No call, no cancel, left you waiting in that restaurant. That's why I came." The emotion departed as her eyes grew heavy. "I'm sorry... I can't keep my eyes open."

Lance stared at Vicki, studying her, making up his mind. He swallowed hard and, having decided, said,

"I can't lie to you either, Vicki. Not when you've listened so patiently. You're so sweet, so understanding, to agree to cut my arm off. I have to tell you the truth. I don't suffer from BIID."

"You..." She could barely hold her head up. Yawning again, slurring her speech, she forced the question out. "You... don't?"

"No. Oh, everything I said was true. Just not true of me. Davina was the one with the disorder. She was obsessed with the belief that her legs needed to be cut off to make her whole. I did it for her. I ended her torment. I made her body... right."

"You..." She tried to wrap her mind around it. "You cut your girlfriend's..."

"...legs off. Yes. She was a new woman after I made her whole. My God, she bloomed! She was so beautiful, so intense, after. And the sex! I amputated a third of her body and she became more woman than I could handle." He laughed at the memory of it, then turned to Vicki. The laughter faded. "Now she's gone. And *I'm* not whole anymore."

Vicki groaned, completely disoriented, but still wanting to be there for Lance. "Oh, you poor, sad, sweet thing."

"You're not repulsed?" he asked in astonishment. "You don't hate me?"

"I don't... understand. But who... am I to... judge? You loved someone... with a rare, awful disea... I don't know... what's wrong... Too much drink."

"No, sweetheart, it's not the drink. It's the *pills* I put in your drink. I've never met anyone like you, Vicki. I made the appointment with your office because of Donna. I'd been following her for weeks because she looked so much like Davina. But she wasn't like Davina. She wouldn't have begun to understand the necessary procedure. She wasn't my type at all. I admit you weren't, either. But it wasn't until after I... after Davina's surgery, I discovered what my type really was."

He rose to his feet.

"Oh, it's going to be great! The freezer is full of ice. I stole a pocket full of suture from Lundgren's office, you picked out the saw yourself, and the bathtub is ready for you."

"Wait," Vicki cried, struggling merely to remain conscious. "Wait. Wait!"

"The wait is over, sweets. Our new lives start tonight." He lifted her, grunting. "Oh, you're heavier than I thought." Lance started down the hall for the bathroom with Vicki in his arms. "I'm not used to carrying a woman that has... *ah*, but don't worry. We'll soon take care of that."

Three

Herb Flay paused at the front door of his tiny basement apartment, looking out and up at the rain and the miniature waterfall descending his small back stairwell. He didn't pause for a rain coat (he didn't own one) or an umbrella (he never would own one). He balled his fist around his car keys, not to lose them in the run, and launched himself out into the storm. Three seconds up the slippery stairs, eight seconds across the back lawn to the community parking lot, four seconds... make that eight... fussing with the lock on the driver's side door of his old Maverick. He dove in and yanked the door closed again with a hollow thud. He was soaked and gasping (for a skinny guy, he wasn't in good shape), but he was out of the rain and on his way. His clothes stuck to his skin, he was squeaking against the vinyl seat, but Flay wasn't about to complain. The Fengriffen Funeral Home and Crematorium had called him back. "Hey," he said aloud, wiping the dripping water from his eyes, "it's a living."

He fired up the old Maverick. He pulled on the lights, turned on the wipers, eased out of the parking lot and into the night. *Yes, sir, it's a living*, he thought.

At least it was once upon a time. Lately, working with the dead hadn't been much of a living.

To say that business had been slow would be the understatement of the century. Business had been awful, horrendous. Only five people had passed away in the whole of the city in the four months Flay had held the job. Three of those five had gone to the competition, the Grimsdyke Funeral Home, on the other side of town. That left two measly services, one a cremation, in four months. No, at that rate helping people to their final rest wasn't much of a living... at all.

The previous morning came back to Herb Flay in a flash.

Marlowe Blake, Flay's boss, had called him into the office and had let him go. Yes, laid him off for lack of work. You could have knocked Flay over with a feather. Mind you, he hadn't been fired. There was no bad blood between them. There was no scene. Nothing was wrong with his work. Flay's work was fine. But in Sturm's Landing, their little part of the world where the only certainties were death and taxes, nobody was dying. Marlowe, with no idea when – or if – he'd be able to call him back, had let Flay go.

"I'm sorry, *ehh*, Herbert," Marlowe had said, in the same hitchy, uncertain way he said everything. "*Ehh.* That's, *ehh*, the way it goes." Flay was devastated. He was by nature a planner and, as far as work was concerned, his plan had gone wrong. His life had fallen apart.

Thus the reason for Flay's excitement, why he jumped for joy when the telephone woke him that stormy morning at one o'clock. Why he was delighted now to be battling the elements in his rickety old Maverick. The Grim Reaper had pulled back his beautiful black cowl, grinned horribly, swung his keenly sharpened scythe, and brought in a couple of sheaves. Flay laughed at the thought. Yes, Death had pointed the razor-tip of a boney metacarpal and, like the phone company, reached out and touched someone. Someones, plural. Two were awaiting removal. Flay howled. Fengriffen's had gotten a call, the call. Late as it was, the call had come in time. Marlowe needed help and, *cha-ching,* Herb Flay had his job back.

Two people had been found dead!

Nobody was doing any squawking, howling, or leaping for joy in the nosy neighbor's Command Post garage. All of them, the gathered cops, firefighters, paramedics, and the Proprietor were as quiet as spiders in a tomb, staring as one in dumb silence at Deputy Maitland. His tale of the poor, unfortunate Vicki Robbins had unsettled them – to say the least. They gawped, each mind doing what it would with the images created by the deputy's description of Lancelot Canning carrying Vicki down his apartment hall toward his waiting tub.

Maitland smiled, sipped his coffee, then broke the silence when he innocently asked, "What?"

"That didn't happen," Lisa Clayton cried out.

"It happened," Maitland assured the paramedic.

"It didn't really happen." She wasn't fooling anyone; her bold declaration was, in reality, a worried question.

"Didn't it?" Maitland asked in return.

"It doesn't matter," Baker, the young firefighter, insisted. "It doesn't matter if it really happened or not. It's a fail. It's the wrong kind of story for what we're doing here."

Maitland looked the question before he asked, "What are we doing here?"

"Killing time," Deputy Grayson told Baker, butting in and sounding, more than he probably intended, like he was coming to his partner's defense. "Telling war stories."

"Telling *spooky* war stories," Maitland said, correcting him and schooling the group. "War stories that fit the setting and the situation."

Lightning flashed, reminding them, if the dull odor of decay permeating the air did not, just what the situation was.

"That's what I mean," Baker said. "Your story was too real. There are all kinds of people out there. One person's routine is another person's crazy. People get over-anxious when a story hits too close to home. It's a horror story, but it isn't entertaining. It's just grueling. An entertaining horror story should be more... well, entertaining. A good horror war story shouldn't be real; it should be surreal."

Thunder rolled. Baker smiled and nodded taking it as the heavens' support for his position.

But he'd lost Deputy Maitland's attention. A new set of lights, churning reds and blues, had appeared in the windows, passed by the garage, and were headed in the direction of the scene. Maitland opened the walk-in and looked into the storm and down the closed-off street. "Speaking of grueling reality. That's the sheriff pulling up." He grabbed his raincoat from its hook.

"You want me to come?" Grayson asked.

"No. You're entitled to a break and you just got here. I'll update the boss and see what he wants us to do. You stay here and. . . " Maitland pointed at Baker, "make sure ol' Blood and Guts here puts his money where his mouth is. I'm sure, being a seasoned veteran, he's got plenty of horrible war stories to properly fit the setting." Maitland grinned, donned his trooper's hat, and vanished into the rain.

The gauntlet had been thrown down. Grayson turned and stared at Baker. The others in the garage followed suit. "You were filling us in on the anatomy of terror?" Grayson chided the young firefighter. "And the proper way to tell a scary story? You say people don't like reality with their horror?"

"They don't," Baker said defiantly. "They like fantasy, an escape. Scary shouldn't be reality. It should hang at the edge of reality. Scary is societal breakdown in a horrific near-future. A future where people have to fend for themselves, where there are no police departments or fire departments left."

That produced a collective stink eye aimed in his direction.

"But," Baker added quickly, "with any luck there are still a few of us around."

"Us?" Grayson asked. "You mean police officers and firefighters?"

"And paramedics!" Clayton put in.

"We've got a better chance than most when the defecation hits the oscillating rotary. We know self-defense, we know First Aid, we know the surrounding villages, towns, and cities."

"And we're bat-shit crazy going in," Reid added. "So no matter what happens, or happened, to society, there would be fewer shocks that we'd need to get over. We've already seen it all."

"So..." Deputy Grayson said, returning his challenging stare to Baker. "Have you got one?"

"A scary story?"

The garage erupted with laughter. "Yeah," the deputy said, shaking his head. "The right kind of story!"

Baker set down his coffee and made a show of cracking his knuckles. "I thought you'd never ask."

Four

He woke with a start, quietly. The former was inescapable; when you lived in a nightmare, startled was the only way to wake. The latter was something he'd trained himself to do; in all things – be quiet. It took him a moment to recognize his surroundings, his bed such as it was, to ground his brain in the there and then (to him, the here and now, of course). Once that was accomplished, add a moment for him to realize he was alone, and another to accept the fact that she had not returned. That was a disappointment.

Wasn't that just about all that life was anymore? Come to think of it, wasn't that pretty much all it had ever been? He laid back to consider the question and couldn't help but ask himself how much (or indeed how little) things had changed. He asked the question again. Wasn't that really all that life had ever been? A disappointment? A barely remembered childhood as a middle child in a family of many siblings. Lost amid the crowd. Too young to have any fun, but old enough the younger ones were his responsibility. And nobody, not mother, not father (when they saw him), not that chin-pinching auntie, could ever remember his name. Admittedly, there were a lot of kids and, admittedly, Milton wasn't a great name but, really, was it that hard to remember? And, though he never objected aloud, he wouldn't have called a dog Miltie. Oh well, what was one more disappointment? Then came a mediocre climb through high school only to find there was neither the money nor the academic acumen to make continuing on to college a road worth taking. After graduation (no party), came an okay job, certainly not a great or even a good job (absolutely not a career), but a working-life-long job that paid the bills. Yes, a disappointment. A too-quick marriage to a high school sweetheart, too much like her demanding know-it-all father. Endless arguments. A fourth anniversary fought through then slept away in the car in the parking lot (she slept alone in the big double bed in the expensive get-away hotel). A fifth anniversary fought through then slept away in the hallway rocker (she slept alone in the big double bed of that expensive Bed & Breakfast). Two wonderful sons she shoved around like chess pawns, teaching each how worthless men were and turning them against their old man. A long drawn out and oh so expensive divorce that in the name of fairness took everything he had (or would have for decades to come). Had enough? So had he. Then and only then came. . .

What the heck was it? A worldwide plague? The apocalypse? A Robert Bloch nightmare? A George Romero wet dream? The night, the year, the life of the living dead? What difference did it make what people called it? It had happened, become a reality, a 4D, interactive, bloodletting, blood drinking, flesh eating, kill or be killed, run like hell, 'to die, to be really dead, dat must be glorious' fright fest in which living human beings were a quickly vanishing commodity. But had things really changed much? Or were there just more disappointments?

And she hadn't returned.

Milton rose to his knees, as quietly as he was able, trying not to rattle the plastic, the papers, the loose metal cans, and peered out. The sun, though partially hidden behind clouds, was up and the day new. But so what? Night or day, it mattered little. It wasn't like in the movies (when there were movies) where the blood-thirsty monsters only shambled out at night. The real ones, the residents, the revenants, could be around at any time, day or night. You were a fool if you didn't look before you showed yourself. So he peered out, taking a good look around. All appeared quiet. He grabbed his bat, poised leaning at the ready, within reach all through the night; *Babe*, his genuine Louisville Slugger. He'd tried an aluminum job at first but had been disappointed; the wobbly metallic *ting* that sounded when it split a shambler's skull had been completely unsatisfying. The solid *crack* of the wooden bat, on the other hand, let him know the job had been accomplished. Anyway, sure that the coast was clear for the moment, Babe in hand, Milton climbed quickly, and as quietly as he was able, up and out of the dumpster where he'd spent his night.

He hustled alone – because she hadn't returned – to the nearest building. It was an abandoned (what building wasn't?) Used Car dealership. He flattened himself against the outside rear wall. You were also a fool if you walked in the open.

Sneaking along the walls of fading buildings and back alleys like an anxious mouse, knowing that at any instant a human-like, but certainly not human, creature might appear out of nowhere and attempt to kill and eat you, was a suspenseful endeavor for the lonely man engaged in it. Surprisingly, it could also be rather tedious. So skip the next little while and the more bland details of survival.

Pick up later in the day when Milton found himself, perhaps by plan, perhaps by instinct, back at his pre-onslaught stomping grounds, the Alpine Guest Haus motel. Of course, in the smack center of northern Illinois, there wasn't anything remotely Alpine about it. It was built on a hill, between two other hills, in the middle of the city. A bike rider wouldn't have been winded getting there from any direction but it was, apparently, Alpine to an earlier owner with big ideas or a vivid imagination. So the Alpine Guest Haus it was.

It was just an old motel; a former knocking shop to local crib babies and home to the errant drug dealer or two before someone (a descendant of the original owner?) with bigger ideas yet poured on the TIF dollars unknowingly supplied by local taxpayers and fixed things up. The hookers, pimps, and a multiplicity of insects, bugs and arachnids, were chased away. New, though perhaps scratched and dented, furniture and mattresses were brought in. A coat of paint was liberally applied, inside and out, and *Voilà*, there stood a low-priced family motel with a conservative clientele of traveling customers ignorant as to the number of venereal diseases and bodies that had once been carried out of the place.

Was Milton judgmental? Hopefully not, at least not unaccountably, for it was also the place where, not long after its cleaning up, he and she had met. She already lived there when Milton moved in and for the longest time, a friendly 'Hello' was all they shared. An occasional opinion about the weather when one or the other was feeling bold. Then it happened, to the world that is, whatever it was that had happened. In no time at all, the zombies overran the place. The small motel was suddenly the Creature Feature resort, Club Dead; the guests no longer guests but appetizers, entrées, and desserts on a block-long buffet. He and the girl had gotten the hell out of there as fast as their legs would carry them, had fortunately run in the same direction, and had, sometime, somewhere along the route, taken hold of each others' hand not to be separated. They'd been together ever since.

Now he was back at the Alpine Guest Haus. Sometime after the plague, Milton noted, someone had troubled to climb the motel's sign and, with bright red paint and a wide brush, renamed the place the 'Madhouse'. Whether or not that was the extent of the decorator's wit can only be guessed. The splintered remains of a ladder laying atop a dried pool of paint and a darker, more impressive dried pool of blood, suggested the sign painter hadn't had time to admire his finished work. Milton couldn't help but think of the horrible end endured by the unknown artist.

Then he was thinking of her again. The girl. They'd been together since the beginning of the end, like Liz Montgomery and Charles Bronson in that old Twilight Zone episode, strangers forced into oneness. Why not? If they weren't in the Twilight Zone, where the heck were they. They? Where the heck was she? And why hadn't she returned?

She'd left him in the dumpster, that night's home away from home, to go and find some edible food. He'd offered, of course, but she had refused. He'd been on the hunt, on guard, at the point for days and was exhausted. She knew it. He knew it too. She wasn't a hanger-on. She wasn't a damsel in distress. She did her part, held up her end of the team. There were any number of stores, fast food joints, residences with shelves of canned goods, refrigerators still operating. And she could move like a cat. He'd remarked several times she moved like a cat. Like him, her fear of the zombies existed, would always exist, but had been dealt with out of necessity. It was her turn to get the food and she went.

It should be mentioned that she had never disappointed Milton. Now, without her, he was feeling strangely... How would she have said it? Discombobulated? And lost. And being lost, he returned alone by unplanned plan, by newly developed instinct, to the place they'd met. Finding it rechristened the Madhouse hadn't cheered him at all.

Then everything got worse.

No sooner had he arrived than he heard a woman screaming... somewhere in the middle of the first floor. He gripped his bat, ran into the open and across the lot – a no-no – and under the balcony overhang to the second floor of rooms, through the breezeway door where the laundry room window came into view. It was from there, the laundry room, that the tumult came. And he saw them.

There were four in the room. Three male creatures – not that their sex mattered a bit. Females were as deadly as males, if not slightly more vicious, and you were out of your freaking mind if you took the once thought of 'gentler sex' into consideration and hesitated in defending yourself. But, for the record, this time it was three male, blood-thirsty, shambling monsters in the laundry room, pinning a still-human girl down on the clothes-folding table.

It wasn't her. It was a girl, but not *the* girl. That was disappointing because Milton had come back to the motel thinking that maybe she... He wanted to see her again so badly. But it wasn't her; it was another girl. He didn't know her and didn't care who she was. Not really. You see, there were so many disappointments it was all but impossible to care anymore. And he didn't. Then the fact really dawned that this girl, the one on the table, beneath the beasts, fighting for all she was worth and losing the battle, wasn't *the* girl – which was a good thing. That meant she might still be alive; might still be out there somewhere! He did not remember the last time something hadn't disappointed him.

He was overcome with a good feeling, a warm feeling, and a sense that a celebration might be in order. Yes, he would celebrate, by rescuing the girl he didn't give a rat's ass about. He put his faithful bat to use and busted the window, hoping the shattering glass would get the creatures' attention. It did. All three turned as one mechanical unit to look, but he wasn't in the window to see any longer. He'd come around, through the door, and already had old Babe over his shoulder ready to deliver.

One of them let go of the girl and took a step in his direction. One step was all it managed. Milton swung the weapon of sanded ash and lacquer right through its left eye orbit, relishing the *crack* as the skull gave way. He cut short his follow-through and brought the bat back in the opposite direction as a second monster put a foot forward. Thirty years earlier, he'd found being a switch-hitter quite a useful trick in Little League. It was even better now. Less than thirty seconds into this so-called fight and there were two shamblers gone and he was down to one. The last one took a hatchet blow straight over the top. That third *crack* was as lovely as the first and the third splash of blood and gray matter as grotesque – yet satisfying – as any he'd ever caused.

But his celebration, his heroics had come too late. The girl was gone. Not physically; she was still there, just dead. Dead and gone. And trouble was, of course, she'd soon be back. He had no choice but to smash her brains out too. That was disappointing.

He searched a while, found no hint of the girl he'd come in search of, and returned for the night – alone – to his dumpster. In the morning, he would start over, again, a new life in that effed-up world, without her. Without her. It started to rain and Milton fell asleep in miserable disappointment.

He was awakened sometime in the middle of the night by cold rain slapping his face and realized that the lid of his dumpster had been lifted open. He woke startled, but quiet. He looked carefully out – into her face. He rubbed the rain and sleep from his eyes. Yes! It was her. For the second time in this new after-life, this post-plague life, he felt elation and a genuine rush of emotion worthy of celebration. Until the lightning flashed and, in the blue-white flicker, he saw that her throat was torn out. He saw the blood of some other sad soul dripping from her lips and chin.

And he saw, behind her and around their dumpster, the twenty-odd creatures she'd brought back with her.

It was terribly disappointing.

Five

Herb Flay pulled into the parking lot of the Fengriffen Funeral Home, passed the gloomy mansion proper, and parked in the back, in front of the four stall garage with an attached crematorium, where the lead cars, hearses, and company van were kept. The titled Fengriffen, Henry Fengriffen, no longer owned the place; he hadn't for years. Henry had shuffled off his mortal coil, and followed a lifetime of clients into the great beyond, long before Flay ever heard of the place. Marlowe Blake, Fengriffen's long-time associate, ran it now; had done since the morning after Henry's game-ending chest grabber. Marlowe had thought it better for business to keep the trusted name.

Why the rather unprofessional sounding 'Marlowe'? Well, he may have been Mr. Blake, Undertaker, to the parade of bereaved customers walking through the mortuary's front door but, to anyone who knew him for more than five minutes, he was just funny ol' Marlowe. He had more twitches, odd eccentric habits, and attended more *Anonymous* groups for varied addictions than any three people – all while trying to foist upon the public, and their nearest relatives, the impression he was a dignified funeral director. Funny or not, had Marlowe been there at that moment, Flay would have kissed his employer on his shiny forehead.

But he wasn't there, and Flay knew he had better get on with the job at hand.

Though it was a beautiful night for death, it was a miserable night for work. The rain fell hard. The lightning flashed. The spooky factor was high, but visibility was crap. Flay hurried inside and up to Marlowe's office, where he grabbed the keys to the van and the note his boss had said he would leave for him (in Marlowe's unmistakable chicken scratch) featuring the address where the bodies had been discovered and from which the removals were to be made. Marlowe had already gone ahead in the Caddy. Alone, Flay ran back down and loaded the van with the needed accoutrement.

The removals, as stated, would take place from a residence in Cedartown. Other than the location, the note added nothing and (over the phone) Flay had been informed of little more. Not only was that not unusual, it was standard for the funeral business. Morticians were always picking up and providing the penultimate conveyance to complete strangers. It was afterward, in meeting with the family, in making the arrangements, during the embalming and cosmetic work, and in giving the dearly departed their final ride, that they got to know the deceased. One by one, their secrets fell like sifted flour; the layers dropped away like a baking artichoke or a peeling onion.

Flay was suddenly hungry. But there was no time to stop. Marlowe, and the removals, awaited him.

The van handled like a broken down lumber truck on its good days. In the storm, Flay knew as he hit the road, it would be something else entirely. It was. Flay choked the wheel as the vehicle shook with the wind, the tires slipped on the pavement, and the windshield wipers managed little better than a tie in their fight with the rain. The lightning flashed white hot. The thunder rolled. Flay cracked open his driver's side window, just a sliver owing to the downpour, for a deep breath of fresh air.

Despite the tension caused by the raging elements, and his need to concentrate on his driving, Flay couldn't help but think about the work ahead – and delight in the notion of the eventual paycheck.

Thank you, Marlowe, his inner voice sang. *Thank you, Death. Thank you, whoever you are, that found the bodies and called.*

It was an ignominious way to meet one's maker, all alone in a dumpster.

Firefighter Baker was just describing that last minute of Milton's life, and the final moment of his story, when the walk-in door was yanked open and two more souls entered the garage. Sandy Lund, the feisty engine driver, in front with Abner Perry, the doughy lead paramedic, following close behind. Lund pulled off her bunker coat, gave the rain water a shake, and glowered at Baker. Perry merely stood dripping, gawping at the group, in horrified disbelief. Neither looked to be fans of thunderstorms or of horror stories. Several of the gathered, startled at their entrance, chuckled nervously as they recognized the pair (and their own silliness at having jumped) and returned their attention to Baker, who was waiting to button the story.

Finally, with the interruption over, with a shake of his head, Baker hit them with the tag. "It was terribly disappointing."

"*Eewww*," Perry cried. "Terribly disgusting, you mean."

"What a way to go," Lund added.

The garage broke up laughing. Baker scowled at the soggy duo, who'd ruined the big ending of his horror tale, and barked, "Don't you like scary stories?"

"Yeah," Lund growled. "Do you know one?"

"No," Perry cried with a dismissive wave of his hand. "I don't do scary."

"Well, go back out in the storm then," Baker said. "Because, in here, we're doing scary."

"Speaking of outside," Grayson said, ending the argument. "What's going on?"

"The coroner just pulled up," Lund replied. "He's with the fire chief and the sheriff now. They're going back into that shit hole. . . " She eyeballed the Proprietor. "S'cuse my French." She returned her attention to the deputy. "They're taking the coroner into the hot zones to examine the rotted bod–" She looked at the Proprietor again, this time with narrowed eyes as his presence was cramping her style. "For a close up look at – the evidence. They'll be a while."

Perry shivered, not from the cold rain, and asked the room, "How's that for horror?"

"That's why we're telling horror stories," Reid said. "To deal with the night."

"It's ghoulish," Perry insisted.

"That's because you're standing on the outside looking in," Clayton told her senior partner. "Come on into the cemetery, Abner."

"Yeah," Baker added. "Pull up a tombstone and tell us a scary war story."

"Just make sure it's better than that last one," Clayton said.

"Wait a minute!" Baker glared. "What was wrong with my story?"

"You said it would be entertaining," the paramedic said. "It was anything but. It was so down beat, I wanted to cut my own throat."

Lund beamed. "Don't let us stop you."

The women traded looks that could kill. The men stayed out of it.

Clayton returned her glare to Baker and went on. "Besides, everyone is sick to death of zombies. You've got to tell a story with some humor in it, even if it's silly. As long as it's scary." She turned again to the engine driver, like a cat to a mouse. "How about you, Sandy? Why don't you dig into that ancient past of yours and tell us a terrifying war story?"

Lund stared daggers, tugged at the front of her bunker pants, and told the skinny blonde, "Dig into this." Then she piled on. "You're the one handing out reviews. Can you do better? Go ahead, Lisa, you tell us a scary war story... If you've got one."

"I've got one," Clayton said with an evil smile. She took a deep breath and let it out slowly. "He heard... moaning."

Six

He heard... moaning.

He heard... a pained and agonized groaning.

But how? He was under water! Wasn't he? Yes... He was somewhere in the cold depths of a black, muddy lake... No, he was rising now; he was racing to the surface. Wait, it wasn't a lake. It was space. Not outer space. Not physical space. But *a* space. What's the word? Figuratively, that was it. He was floating... in a space in his head. He was... racing toward consciousness.

Then... geez! Someone screamed! It was a short, startled bleat... and then it was gone; it was cut off as quickly as it erupted. It scared the living hell out of him and... Wait... He suddenly realized it was him! He had screamed. He couldn't catch his... He was breathing quickly now, panting like an overheated dog, quite involuntarily and, as consciousness became cognizance, he couldn't help himself. He needed to scream again. "God. My God!"

His panting was doing nothing. He was hyperventilating. He couldn't catch his breath. He couldn't get any air, couldn't breathe! *Stop it*, he told himself. He had to stop or he was going to pass out again.

He... had... to slow... his breathing. He took air in through the nose, held it. He exhaled through the mouth. Again, in through the nose. Out through the mouth. Better. That was better. Still, something was wrong. He felt trapped, unable to move. He couldn't... Wake up. He had to wake up. "I'm sick!"

Why couldn't he move? Why couldn't he wake? Where the hell was he? It was dark. So very dark. How did he get there? He had to think; he had to remember. Last week. *Yes, yes,* he thought, *it started last week... with the room next door... and... the lady of the evening.*

His name was Eric Landor. He lived in room 303, upper, rear, of a shabby little motel in the middle of nowhere. He was a writer of *hoary gorys*, those fog-laden, trope-filled tales his publisher and a scant few readers referred to as thrillers or murder mysteries, and, when asked, he replied that he was moderately successful at it. By moderately successful he meant that, while few knew his name, he was able to afford food, clothes, and the room rent in a shabby little motel in the middle of nowhere. Motel living had its advantages for a fellow like Landor, no utility bills, clean linens, and hot, black coffee near at hand twenty-four-seven. Of course it had its disadvantages as well. Chief among them... fate picked your neighbors; and upstanding citizens lived in homes, not motels.

The truth was that daily, sometimes weekly, all of life's losers, down and outs, pimps, druggies, sluts, and escapees checked into the rooms on either side of his, and the room below him, and temporarily called them home. To those temporal nests they came, in them they stayed, and from them they went while Landor had no choice but to hear – and occasionally see – slices of what should have been their private lives nakedly displayed. They made up an unending parade of human debris. They laughed too loud on Saturday nights. They prayed too loud on Sunday mornings. They drank. They fought. They rutted like insane weasels.

Groan, groan, groan. Thump, thump, thump. Bang, bang, bang. Scream.

You probably understand what he was hearing.

The latest one was a lady (and by that Landor meant, of course, a lady of the evening) who'd been in room 304 – the room to the west of his – for five days and, more pointedly, nights. Landor had never seen her; they didn't keep the same hours. But he heard her... and her guests. Every night, several times a night; the same room, the same girl, and each time a different guy – though they made similar noises.

Groan, groan, groan. Thump, thump, thump. Bang, bang, bang. Scream.

Followed always by a silence that, pardon the cliché, was deafening.

And, in regard to the frequency of her dalliances, the lady absolutely blew Landor away, he was in awe. In the writer's extended stay at the motel he'd seen some goers, but she was relentless. Coming and going, going and coming, only to start it all over again. The thumping, the banging, and the screaming. The way he remembered it, it had been one hell of a week to say the least.

Then came the night he actually saw her...

Landor was minding his own business, his usual business, killing the latest fictional incarnation of his ex-wife, tapping away at his latest novel, at his usual table in the far corner next to the decorative but non-functioning fireplace in the motel's drab lobby, when the electronic door chime sounded and she came in. He paused, then pushed the 'Reset' button in his brain, changing the 'she' to a 'they' in his thoughts, as there were two of them. The lady of the evening had a guy in tow.

But, truth be told, Landor didn't care about him. Whoever he was. His attention went to where it belonged, on the lady. Landor wondered if he'd be a politically incorrect, misogynistic pig in a cheap suit, if he admitted to himself that she looked good enough to eat?

"Guot eve-e-nink."

That's what she said. Good evening. But she didn't talk, she purred. And, while Shakespeare preferred words trippingly off the tongue, Landor would have been willing to bet the old boy would have been okay with her delivery. He certainly was. She had a thick, eastern European accent (Serbian, or Hungarian, or Russian. He was a writer, what do he know?). It was delicious; slow like dripping honey.

Then she said, "Is a beau-ti-ful night, yesss?" And Landor fell in love with snakes.

She wore short shorts, a halter top, a lace jacket, net stockings, and knee-high boots with stiletto heels; all as black as the night. Her jewelry – crystalline, crimson, and jade – had no business being real in a motel like that, but sure looked it; all set in silver accoutrement. She had a blood red tramp stamp on her stomach that Landor couldn't make out from that distance. Regardless of what it was or how it read, it screamed 'Slut!' in any language.

"My key. It's not verk-ink." She slid the malfunctioning key card across the counter. Then, at Louise's request (Louise Saville was the night clerk working the front desk), the dark beauty produced a license.

"Adrea Spedding. Yessss," she said, agreeing with Louise she was who the license said and, at the same time, proving her right to occupy room 304.

Not that her name mattered. Not that the flavor of the hour, the nervous fellow beside her (Landor decided to call him 'John'), mattered. Not that anything mattered to the writer. It was sexist, he knew. It was vulgar. But Landor just kept staring at that dark, foreign beauty, dressed like a gutter crib-baby from a bad sitcom, murmuring under his breath, "God, that looks good enough to eat!"

The door chime repeated its three-note song as they left. Landor closed his laptop, hurriedly threw his stuff into his duffle, and made a pathetically unconvincing excuse to Louise for his rapid departure, which was childish and entirely guilt-driven. (She didn't ask and he didn't owe her one.) Then he quickly and unobtrusively followed the couple as Adrea-whatever hurriedly directed John to her room.

Landor was almost ashamed to remember what he did next. But he did it all the same. He leaned against the wall in his room, and listened from his side like some sleazy pervert, while Adrea-dark and John-dork groaned, thumped as they upset the furniture, banged on the wall, and, as usual, worked themselves up to a scream.

But geez! This time, it was a hell of a scream!

Despite his perverse enjoyment, Landor was shaken to the core. Something awful had happened in that room next door. The writer couldn't recover quickly enough to hurry to the front office and complain like the hypocrite he was. "There's something going on in room 304."

"What do you mean?" Louise wasn't the sharpest knife in the drawer.

Landor made three attempts to subtly get the message across before exasperation set in. "For the fourth time, Louise," he barked at her, "I don't know what I mean. I'm not in room 304, I'm in 303. But they've been thumping the heck out of my wall. . . "

"Well, Mr. Landor, it's. . . You know, it's a motel." Apparently, Louise didn't think he was all that sharp either.

"I'm not talking about that kind of thumping, Louise. Do you think I'd be up here if I was talking about that kind of thumping? Someone. . . doing something. . . Not that kind of thing, but a different kind of thing, banged. . . I don't mean banged, I mean thumped, on my wall and then screamed."

She stared at him like he was a bug. And, Landor had to admit, her complete lack of curiosity was doing nothing to alter his opinion of her general dullness. "Louise?" he said, trying to rouse her. "This is where you say, I'll call the police."

"I can't call the police, Mr. Landor."

"There's the phone, Louise." He pointed over the counter. "Pick up the receiver. Push the nine once, and the one twice."

51

"I'm not allowed." That's what she said. She went on to explain, "Lucy (that's the front desk manager) says it's bad for the motel's reputation to have the police here." Then, because she was convinced Landor was dense, she repeated, "So we're not allowed to call them."

Though he was almost certain he would regret it, Landor launched into a debate. "What if a situation comes up where you need them?" he asked.

"Like what?"

"Like... the situation that's come up, Louise."

"Oh, she didn't say. She just said, don't call the police."

Landor was right, he regretted it. "That's a tremendous policy." He sighed then, taking a new tact, said, "All right, Louise, give me a key to the room."

"I can't give you a key to the..."

"Louise, something bad has happened in room 304. It's not my imagination. I've asked you to call the room..."

"There's no answer!"

"Right, which, if you think about it, strengthens my argument something bad has happened. I've asked you to check the room..."

"I can't leave the desk!"

"Right. I've asked you to call the police..."

"I'm not allowed to call them!"

"Right. So... I'm offering to check the room for you." Honestly, like a bug. Landor was half afraid she'd stick a pin through him and put him in her science fair project. "Louise? Do you want Lucy to find a hooker's corpse in room 304 tomorrow morning?"

"NO! But I don't want to find one either!"

"If I check now, she might not be a corpse yet. Wouldn't it reflect better on you if you saved her life? Or, if it's too late, wouldn't it be better to find a warm, fresh corpse as opposed to a cold, stiff, seven-hour-old corpse?"

She hesitated. Then, slowly, the Ferris wheel in the carnival she called a head started to go around. "O-kay. . ."

"Okay!"

Landor slid the duplicate key card that Louise had given him into the lock to the door of room 304. He heard the acknowledging beep. The pad beside the handle flashed green. The lock snicked.

The mystery writer didn't know what he expected to see or hear when the door came open. But what he saw was darkness and what he heard was nothing. He didn't know what he expected to smell – the heavy odor of pot, the musk of human coupling, the metallic tinge of spilled blood. Any of those would have been better than the odor he got. Room 304 smelled of the unmistakable, unrivaled stench of human decay. Repulsed but, with a writer's often-misguided curiosity, unable to retreat, he entered the room. Two steps beyond the threshold the door – on spring hinges – closed behind him.

He groped the wall for the light switch, found the cover missing, the switch exposed and dangling on stiff wires. *Click-click, click-click.* The lights weren't working.

Alarmed, he found himself backing away from the displaced switch (and foolishly the door) into the room. He strained, scanning the blackness for any sign of anything until... His progress was arrested when his head collided with something hanging from the ceiling. It was huge with a surface as rough in places as dried papier-mâché and as sticky in others as molasses. Though he could just see its bulbous outline, it was instantly obvious to even his disoriented brain that he had run into some kind of cocoon.

He backed away in horror. Only to run into another like-object hanging several feet further into the room. From there, again... another. And another beyond that.

"My God!"

The whole room was full of those hellish things. Cocoons... reeking with the odor of decaying human flesh. But where... Where was the lady of the evening?

Then Landor heard the strangest sound, all but indescribable; a wet fishing line unwinding, a harp string in mid-pluck; perhaps more a vibration than a sound. For he turned, not when he heard it, but when he felt it.

His eyes had adjusted, somewhat, to the dark. He could see a brilliantly woven orb web where there should have been ceiling and, suspended from its center above his head by a silvery, silken thread... was the lady of the evening. The crimson design – the tramp stamp – on her stomach was visible now and, even without the light, he could see it was not a tattoo. It was a natural mark in the shape of an hour-glass.

Landor screamed. He screamed! HE SCREAMED! Or thought he did.

For it soon occurred to him that his mouth was hanging open, and great gobs of air were escaping through it, but he wasn't making a sound. Merely gaping like a landed trout. He had no voice. He couldn't scream. The thing on the ceiling, the lady, was... Landor backed away to the wall... He clenched his fist, though something... something inside of him was fighting, trying to hold him back, to prevent him... But he forced himself. He raised his fist and he thumped... and banged against the wall, trying to alert someone, anyone, to his desperation, to his horror.

And the horror closed in.

He banged again. Oh, God, his mind was screaming, would no one hear him? Would no one help him? And then it dawned on Landor. Louise was right, he wasn't all that sharp. The wall bordered his own room. He hadn't come to anyone's aide when he'd heard the banging, the thumping, the screaming... and nobody was coming to his.

The dark lady drew near. My God, my God, Landor was suddenly thinking. The lady was so... beautiful...

And now Landor had resurfaced from some unconscious place.

"God. My God!" he whispered.

He felt trapped, unable to move. He couldn't...
Wake up. He had to wake up. Sick...

"I'm sick!"

But where was he now? It was dark. So very dark. But... wait... What was that? They were lights, dull, defused; eight red lights in a cluster, glowing softly as if filtered through cheese cloth. No, silk; woven silk. NO! Spun silk... before his eyes. Thread... A spider's thread woven before his eyes, spun round his body; suspending him there in room 304. With eight red lights, glowing in the dark, approaching stealthily, and gaining definition as they drew near. Hissing! Landor heard hissing... And the lights, slowly approaching, he now saw were not lights at all, but eyes. The eyes... of the lady of the evening.

She wrapped her arms around him. He was hers, locked, delighted in the thrill of her embrace. She pulled him and he followed gladly, without resistance, with a feeling of falling, in eager anticipation... To the bed, he assumed, or the floor perhaps, or maybe even to Hell. Landor didn't know and he didn't care. Then, sweetness in life, she wrapped her legs around him.

Her breath, and his, were one heated cloud. She whispered, "Yes. Yessssss!"

Then... she wrapped... her other legs around him.

And, again, she wrapped... two more legs around him.

Her fangs had a delicious sting! A burning... God, a burning that raced through his body. Sweat burst from every pore as the pungent odor of hot iron, the smell of his own flowing blood filled his nostrils. Her gasps... mixed with his screams. Oddly the screams, even as he voiced them, didn't seem like they were his... And, as darkness enveloped him, he could feel the warm wetness of her saliva as it dripped, soaking his silk cocoon. He could see her licking her bright red lips. And through that horrid hissing noise she was making, she was also saying... something. Landor couldn't make it out. She was... Wait! He could hear her now. Yes, he could hear her!

"Ohhhhhh, Gott! Dat looks good enof to eat!"

Seven

Flay wrestled the steering wheel, fought to see ahead through the black rain; he was wishing he was there, hoping he would soon be there. He turned to the wide rear compartment for a quick glance at the equipment he'd brought; the items he'd been specifically asked to bring. He'd checked it all when he loaded it, of course. But Marlowe, on top of being a goof of a funeral director, was paranoid too, which made his employees paranoid out of necessity. Flay knew he'd be asked immediately upon touchdown if he had everything, and Marlowe would have a stroke if he so much as hesitated in his answer.

With his eyes darting from the road ahead to the compartment behind, and back again, he quickly took inventory. One collapsing wheeled stretcher. Only one was necessary, regardless of how many bodies there were, they'd be removed one at a time. The dead were a patient lot. One stretcher, check. Two body bags, the thick black rubber ones. Marlowe had made it clear. "*Ehh.* Herbert, I can't emphasize this enough," he'd said. "The regular bags will, *ehh,* not do. Bring two of the heavy ones." Two deluxe bags, check. Latex surgical gloves. "Not, *ehh,* just two pair. *Ehh.* Bring the box." One box of gloves, check. And towels. "*Ehh.* Bring plenty!" Okay. One large pile of towels, check.

Glad for the work, Flay asked no questions. If they were heading into battle, so be it. He brought the heavy artillery as instructed. Marlowe would have nothing to squawk about.

It was the new norm in the garage Command Post; the story over, the firefighters, the cop, and the paramedics stared at each. Nobody said a word. Nobody even breathed. Then Sandy Lund broke the silence. "A spider woman? O – M – G! What kind of hokey nonsense is that?"

"It's disgusting nonsense," Abner Perry cried, writhing as if he was covered in the eight-legged menaces himself. "That's what it is, disgusting. *Eeeww.*"

Clayton smiled. "Liked it, huh?"

"No," Lund said, with a sneer. "It was stupid and unbelievable. Nothing that damn crazy happens without a reason. Crazy is all right for a campfire story, but there has to be a reason for the crazy."

"Maybe you can do better, Sandy?" Clayton hissed the question. "I asked you to tell one before. So go ahead. Tell one."

The engine driver folded her arms defiantly and twisted her lips in a combination frown and grimace. She studied the group around her: Clayton, the pillow princess paramedic; fellow firefighters Reid and Baker, the older winking his approval, the younger nodding his support; Grayson the deputy, studying her in return like she was a DUI suspect about to perform a roadside test; and Perry and the Proprietor, standing together like Tweedledee and Tweedledum, the paramedic sweating in fear, the garage owner sweating in something looking too damn near lust to want to think about. She studied the inside of her eyelids for a moment. *What the hell,* Lund thought, *why not?* She nodded once, then growled, "I've been bleeding from the vagina for two weeks."

The Proprietor made a gulping noise as if he'd swallowed his tongue. Baker spit his coffee. Grayson did a double-take, grinned, and said, "Too much information." Clayton merely mouthed, 'Wow.'

"No," Lund shouted. "Not me, you rat bastards!" She glared the group down. "I'm telling a story!"

"Sure," Reid said, as if trying to calm an agitated mental patient. "Sure."

"You gonna let me tell my story?" Lund demanded.

"I can't wait," Baker said, dabbing at the coffee on his shirt.

"We're all ears," Clayton added, sneering again.

"Right," Lund said. "Then listen up."

Eight

"I've been bleeding from the vagina for two weeks."

That's what she told Max Berg.

Max sighed under his breath and shook his head in dismay. Why him? What did he look like, a doctor? He wasn't a doctor; he was a nobody, he was a chemical technician. A laid-off chemical technician, at that. Did he look like he could help her? Did he look like he even cared? Because he didn't, not one bit. He was a stranger, that was all. A complete stranger, suffering through the coldest winter on record, shivering in his seat, just minding his own business riding the city bus. Then this old lady, pink and powdery with a bee-hive of silver and blue hair, in a musty gray tweed coat, led by a chilly blast, climbed aboard. Trailing melting snow, she made her way down the aisle, eyeballed the place beside him, ignoring a half-dozen other seats just as empty, and sat her boney biscuits down. She pulled off a glove, cleared her throat with a slight cough into a skeletal paper-skinned fist, and declared, "I've been bleeding from the vagina for two weeks."

What could he say to that? What could anybody say to that? Nothing. And he didn't. Max had been at it long enough to know it was all part of riding the bus. Expect the unexpected. That was his maxim for bus-riding. Expect the unexpected, and anything imaginable after that.

While there were exceptions (there were exceptions to everything), there were usually two kinds of people that rode the bus: those that were going to beg you for money and, worse, those that were going to try to get into your business. Bastards. No, it wasn't politically correct. But Max knew nothing about politics; he didn't even vote, so what did he care? The people that made it their business to decide what was and was not acceptable in public didn't ride the frigging bus.

Mind you, Max had no trouble admitting that those two kinds of riders, like ice cream and sherbet, came in a wide variety of flavors. There were the sleepers. Max didn't even remember the last time he rode when there wasn't some slumped degenerate avoiding the cold outside by sleeping on the bus. Why not? Life was so much simpler when you were unconscious. There were the wheelchair people. Don't get him wrong, Max had nothing against them. There but for the grace of God, you know. But the stop to pick up some guy in a wheelchair took forever, and they covered the floor in snow, ice, and mud, and their chairs took up four seats, and you couldn't get around the damned things. Whoever created the mass transit system patted themselves on the back for helping the handicapped, but they didn't ride the frigging bus either.

That wasn't all. There were the book worms, the oglers, the secret eaters (ignoring the signs and sneaking bites from overstuffed pockets full of disallowed food), the ear bud people, the texters, the I'm-gonna-scream-on-my cell phoners, the little old things, the quiet ones, the creepy ones; all kinds of riders. But if they did anything other than just ride, if they spoke to you, Max knew, you were in for douchebaggery. They wanted money, or they wanted to ask you something that was none of their damn business, or they wanted to tell you something you didn't want to know. Just like Granny Pink Powder in the seat beside him.

There were a lot of douche-bags rode the bus. But, Max knew too, *that* sword cut both ways, because the city went out of its way to encourage doucheness, if you asked him. The downtown terminal was full of threatening signs, on the soda machines, the bathroom doors, and on the windows at the information and ticket booths, 'Don't do that', 'Don't do this', 'Do this and these will be taken from you', 'Do that and the cops will be called', all posted within grinning distance of a too old, or too young, or too skinny, or too fat rent-a-cop carrying a firearm, patrolling the terminal, and thinking he's God's gift to law enforcement. The city treated their riders, their customers, like crap. They got what they gave.

Point was, nothing against nobody but Max knew it was a good idea to keep an eye out when he rode the bus. Because two kinds of people, meaning all kinds of people, rode the bus. It didn't have to be midnight for criminals to scurry out from beneath their rocks, and it didn't have to be Halloween for the monsters to come out. The key to riding safe, to not being hassled, was to be a chameleon, to fit in so you didn't stick out. That was how you kept a low profile, avoided being seen, and avoided trouble on the bus. Yeah, in that concrete jungle, especially on the buses, Max was a chameleon.

That day, Max was on the Number 7 route, the Main Street Express. The Main Street Express ran the west-east length of town in a straight line from the downtown terminal, past the Polish-American Hospital (they treated everybody, but the city's Poles started it eighty years ago pitching in a dollar a-piece to break ground), past mid-town, past the Catholic Hospital (nick-named Saint Agony by folks didn't get the service they thought they deserved), and on to Wally World (the big department store) at the end of the drag. There it did a careful U-turn in the parking lot of the mom and pop sub sandwich shop, taking care not to slide off the ice-covered road into the ditch on the way out, and returned the opposite direction.

Max was being a chameleon on the Express when the old lady got on, took the seat beside him, and began dispensing 'too much information'. Okay, sometimes being a chameleon didn't keep everyone from pestering you but, thankfully, she took herself, and her seeping plumbing, right back off at the Polish hospital and good luck to the old biddy. He thought he'd catch a breather but, turned out, being a chameleon wasn't working worth a damn that day. Right away, as the old lady shuffled off, son of a gun if her replacement didn't step on.

This guy had a mop of wild black hair over six feet in the air, two days' growth of spotty beard, dark (dirty brown or maybe gray) patched pants, and a quilted green winter coat torn almost to rags. He was huge and the bus dipped like a homemade pier when his three-hundred plus pounds stepped on. He barreled down the aisle like a thrown snowball, right at Max, bringing a rush of frigid air with him.

It definitely wasn't the chameleon's day because the guy pivoted on his size-fourteen sneakers and, despite a third of the seats being empty, plopped his big ass right down on the seat the old girl had just vacated. Breathing in deep rales like a dying asthmatic and smelling like smashed garlic, his girth spilled back into the aisle on one side and onto Max on the other. That only partly described him.

He was a man of color, but nothing like anyone Max had seen before. He was a mix of earth tones, a deathly gray (at his wrists, ears, and on his face), a dull brown (at his eyes, lips, and throat), with faded yellow all around like nutrient deficient dirt, like a worn and neglected relic pulled from a chest in Grandma's attic. He didn't have a color so much as he gave off an aura, as if his skin was less a protective covering for his massive body than it was a barometer of the feelings churning within. His bulk suggested overabundance but everything else about him cried of loneliness, need, and want.

It won't surprise you that Max, for the most part, was unmoved, and that's putting it lightly. To be blunt, the fat bastard stank and was swamping him with his disgusting overlap, and it was all Max could do not to demand he move elsewhere. But making a scene went against his chameleon rule. He bit his tongue instead, figuratively that is, as one did on the bus. Odd things often happened and they were usually best observed without comment.

Then, speaking of odd things, *it* happened.

Glistening with melted snow, the fat man turned silently toward him, smiled a friendly smile, then lifted his heavy eye lids showing wet but dull blue eyes. In an instant, his left eye dilated; the iris disappeared and the whole surface of the eye became one huge black pupil. It stared unblinking at Max, like a reptile from a tree branch, and right into his soul. His unchanged right eye, meanwhile, acting quite independently of the other, rotated away to look to the front of the bus. So startled was Max by what he'd seen, he didn't notice at first the quick, sharp punch to his side just above his hip. When he did he bit his tongue again, this time literally, to keep from screaming.

It wasn't that he felt any pain; whatever it was that had happened was all but painless. But it was a hell of a surprise, coming as it did out of left field. The fellow beside hadn't seemed to move at all and certainly hadn't raised a hand. Max hadn't expected a thing. A moment later, after the initial shock, he felt it more clearly and realized it wasn't a fist at all. Nor was it a weapon as he'd define one. It was some sort of living appendage, a part of the fat man, a sharp-ended tentacle reaching from one of the holes in his coat and impaling Max through his side. He hadn't just been punched or stabbed. That would have been bad enough, but Max could feel the tentacle pushing in, undulating and twisting, deeply invading him.

Yet Max felt no pain. Somehow the fat man, the thing, had suddenly and inexplicably anesthetized him. Max couldn't utter a sound and couldn't have cried out had he wanted. He managed one quick turn of the head, a look in the stranger's direction, before an otherworldly paralysis took possession of him. Then he couldn't move at all.

"You have many questions," the fat man said, without moving his lips or speaking aloud. Max heard it only in his head, but he heard it all the same. "I know. You are afraid and you have many questions. I regret there will be time to answer but a few. I am from a small, relatively near planet, just outside the orbit of your Pluto; our planet's name corresponds with nothing in your language. Trust me, it does not matter to you. How I came to your world is a lengthy story and also outside your concern."

The bus vibrated and stuttered down its route, past ice laden trees, houses, stores, and around a fender-bender witnessed by tobogganers and a coal-eyed snowman. The air brakes hissed as riders boarded. The bells rang as others called for their stops. Everyone aboard was about his or her own business. No one paid Max or the fat man the slightest attention.

"We are not new to your Earth," the alien said. "Many of my society have come before; many will follow. We are amused by your motion pictures with their superior aliens bringing sacred truths and desperate warnings to your leaders. We are the *real deal*, as your people would say, and have learned the very best start to one of our missions is to quietly purchase a bus pass."

The alien smiled. His black eye stared unblinking. "We have no interest in re-engineering your society. We're not trying to prevent your polluting or conquering the universe; as if you could." The alien laughed heartily without the slightest change to his facial expression. "We have no message for you. We are here to feed; independently for survival and communally for our society. Your life essences, your blood and tissues, are feeding me now."

Max felt it. As they silently rode, him sinking in his seat, held upright only by whatever it was protruding from the stranger's side and into him, he was being drained of everything that made him a vital human being.

"Your emotions meanwhile," the alien continued, "will feed my world. Like the classic tastes sought by master chefs of your planet, our society is sustained by classic emotions: sweet love, pungent hatred, salty strength, sour disappointment, astringent retribution. Our agents have the capacity to instantly sense and target individuals with personalities ripe with specific emotions, to collect those emotions in all their aspects, and transfer those feelings home for communal consumption. As you have no doubt guessed," the creature said, with a roll of its left eye, "I collect bitter."

Max hadn't the ability to protest or the strength to swear. Soon he lost the desire. His consciousness grew fuzzy. His touch with reality began to slip away. The winterscape seemed to race by, the blocks passed outside the windows as if the city were moving and the bus standing still. Though he knew it was early morning, it began to look like dusk approaching.

Max wasn't the only one feeling it. Changes were taking place in the fat man too. He breathed softer and more freely as he fed. His wheeze disappeared. The sickening odor of garlic went with it. The yellows, grays, and sullen browns faded from his skin, replaced by a glistening champagne-white with a lively green around the eyes and at his lips and nose. It was as if a new creature inside him was being released; vicious, yes, but young, bold, and healthy.

"Yes," the alien confessed, "I've been forced to judge you. I can only apologize for the illogical conundrum that creates, but your limited language has no words to precisely describe who or what I am or precisely what I do. I admire a number of your words that brush the definition: traveler, collector, eraser. There is a term I particularly like, given the emotion I am obligated to collect: street sweeper. Forgive me too that I do not feel for you. It would be a waste; humans like you are dead already. I feel, instead, for those of my brethren obligated to collect your lovers of life."

Before either of them knew it, with a hiss of air brakes, the bus had pulled up at the stop outside of the Catholic hospital.

"Ah," the alien said in Max's barely cognizant mind. "Timed perfectly. I am finished with you and this, as your people say, is where I get off. My world thanks you and I thank you. You were delicious." With a slurp his tentacle was withdrawn and vanished back into his torn coat. Max slumped against the window while the traveler rose from his seat and slapped his side in satisfaction.

The bus heaved with relief as he stepped off the platform and into the snow. Two waiting passengers, eager for some warmth, paying him no mind whatever, climbed aboard. The alien lumbered slowly around and behind the *Bus Stop* kiosk.

Through barely-opened unfocused eyes, through the fogged bus window, through the frosted plexiglass wall of the kiosk, the dying Max saw the traveler walk away and realized that, as far as chameleons were concerned, he'd been a rank amateur. For he saw that, as he went, the alien began to transform. His whole monstrous body shrank down and in. His meaty hands, already hanging low, depended even further and took on the shapes and colors of overfull shopping bags. His tangle of black hair became a maroon babushka, his torn coat gathered to accommodate his thin, hunched self, stretched to his ankles as it mended and turned gray-white. He... She now, for the traveler had become an octogenarian bag-lady in sagging hose and orthopedic shoes, started slowly up the salted sidewalk in the direction of St. Agony on the hill.

None of the book worms, oglers, secret eaters, ear bud wearers, texters, cell phone shouters, old things, the quiet, or the creepy aboard the bus paid the departed alien or his transformation the slightest attention. Neither did they pay any attention to Max Berg as he took his final breath or to the shell he left behind. Why should they? In the winter, there were always people sleeping on the bus.

Nine

Flay saw white pinpoints ahead. He leaned forward over the steering wheel and strained, staring through the rain-spattered windshield, between the sweep of the wipers, as the lights of Cedartown grew larger and brighter at his approach. He slowed for the well-known police speed trap on the outskirts, though he doubted it was currently in operation, and eased slowly into the village. He passed the little bar, the Cedar Stop, on the right and the little barber's salon, the Cedar Shop, on the left. Then he made a left hand turn off the main drag. He slowed two streets down, wanting to be certain of the directions, and started a right-hand turn onto a street without a lighted corner, curb, or shoulder.

He cut the corner too sharply and, without being aware, drove the van off the road. The wet grass and mud of the small ditch didn't help him but did aid the slide. A last turn of the steering wheel, too late to do any good, was the cherry on his crap sundae. The van's tail-end slid further, the passenger's side rear tire struck the lip of the cement culvert draining away a torrent of rain water. The tire's sidewall tore and the van's rear end sat down to cry.

Herb Flay knew just how it felt.

Again, those gathered in the garage stood in post-story stillness. Some, Grayson chief among them, looked at the others for reactions. Some, Perry chief among them, were unable to look anywhere at all and merely stared at the concrete floor, freaked out. As before, Sandy Lund broke the silence. "We found him just like that, looking like he was sound asleep, dead as a stone, sitting there on that crosstown bus."

Reid snorted. Baker laughed out loud.

"Laugh, numb nuts," Lund told them. She pointed to the rain covered windows. "The Chameleon is still out there."

The walk-in door opened and Lisa Clayton, the nearest to it, jumped and shrieked. Everyone in the place had a laugh at her expense as a rain-soaked parade came marching in, the stone-faced sheriff in the lead, the gruff-looking old country coroner right behind, and the tired-looking fire chief on his heels. The mountainous ladder truck driver, Paul Henderson, brought up the rear, slipping through the doorway opening sideways to fit, with a firefighter's air pack dangling heavily from each hand.

Recovered from her shock and only moderately redder than before, Clayton grabbed the door and held it open. Reid and Baker, knowing where their bread was buttered, grabbed an air pack each. The relieved Henderson flexed his fingers to get the blood flowing again. The Proprietor cleared plates and cups from his makeshift table to give the equipment, harnesses, regulators, and fresh air bottles a place to rest.

The remainder of the gathered, their laughter spent, looked on in muted anticipation. What they saw on the faces of their fearless leaders was rare and hard to describe. All four of the new arrivals were hardened veterans, but all four, as they shook off the rain, looked shaken to their cores.

"Put away the questioning looks," the sheriff told them. "Two dead, for a long time."

"Nothing more to add," the coroner added, "until they're autopsied. And nothing more to do here until we get them where the posts are to be conducted."

Lund put down her coffee cup, raring to go. "Need help loading them?"

The coroner, white wings of wispy hair fluttering on his mostly bald head, now his hat had been lifted off, ogled the engine driver through rain-spattered glasses like she was insane. "I'm not loading them. I called Fengriffen's the moment I got the call. They can have them. I'll do the autopsies at their funeral home."

"So we hurry up and wait some more?"

"Shouldn't be too long. Marlowe's already here." That needed no explanation, everyone in the emergency business knew the local morticians and, even if they didn't, they knew funny ol' Marlowe. The coroner was going on, "He pulled up when we were headed over. He's sitting in his Cadillac by the house, right in the heart of the stink, waiting for his help to get here with their van."

"Speaking of sitting in the stink," the fire chief said, eyeballing Reid and Baker. "Sorry, boys, but it's your turn in the barrel. Go keep an eye on that expensive equipment of ours, will you." It was neither a question nor a request. Reid and Baker gathered their gear and started dressing for the rain.

The sheriff, meanwhile, turned to Deputy Grayson. "Your colleague could probably use some company too. He's sitting in his squad and putting on a solid front but, if you ask me, something's got him a little spooked right now."

Another laugh, more nervous than hearty, passed between those gathered in the garage.

"We were telling scary war stories," Baker explained, pulling on his bunker coat.

"And you're suggesting you scared my deputy?" the sheriff asked.

"He only heard his own. He scared himself. But some of them since have been pretty..." Baker searched for the word.

"Scary?" Reid offered. Everyone laughed again.

"Yeah, I guess so." Baker's blush now matched Clayton's.

"They're disgusting," Abner Perry exclaimed, with no willingness to join the party atmosphere of the forced gathering. "They're disgusting and evil."

"Oh, Abner," Clayton said. "You're making too much of it. Besides, that last one wasn't scary, disgusting, or evil. It was just idiotic."

"You mean mine?" Lund barked, squaring off, her fists balled.

"Yes, yours," the little blonde shot back, with no sign of intimidation. "That's no way to tell a horror story. An alien on a bus. What a load of crap. And you said mine wasn't believable!"

The sheriff and fire chief watched the building argument with wary eyes; neither wanting to get in the middle of it, both hoping it would lead nowhere. The other emergency workers took it in without emotion. The Proprietor looked on with silent, but palpable, delight.

"Ladies," the fire chief finally said, tamping the thick air with his hand. "Let's keep it to a roar." Then, to prove it was no big deal, he returned his attention to Reid and Baker, pointed at the door, and sent them on their way.

Finished laying out the air pack harnesses, Henderson stepped to the closed overhead door and, through the streaked windows, watched the firefighters go. The raincoat clad Grayson followed and caught them up. The ladder driver stared as all three figures became unreal shapes, eerie silhouettes when the red, blue, and yellow lights of the emergency vehicles flickered, gray ghosts when lightning flashes illuminated the rain, and invisible in-between when the darkness swallowed them whole.

"You don't need aliens," Henderson whispered.

"What?" The Proprietor was suddenly at his side offering a cup of coffee. "I'm sorry. I don't mean to pry. But... What did you say?"

"I said, you don't need aliens," Henderson repeated. He lifted his voice to address the group, but kept his eyes on the dark storm outside. "You don't need space aliens to find horror. There's more than enough to terrify in the darkness."

"You mean at the scene," their host asked, with something akin to a grin. "In that house?"

"I mean in this world. Out there." The ladder truck driver turned from the window to take in the group.

"You know what's out there? Evil... And you can't just look at it and see it for what it is. Because evil looks just like us."

He studied the group: the alert sheriff, the now curious coroner, the queasy lead paramedic and his pixie partner, his old friend the fire chief, his long-time colleague, Lund, and the ever-giddy Proprietor with his bottomless coffee pot and his twisted sense of delight. Henderson asked them all, "You want to hear a story? About another group of firefighters in another place and time; a horror story?"

Ten

The fire engine driver and his lieutenant could see the glow in the night sky three minutes after Engine Two left the station. The veteran firefighter, in the jump seat behind the driver, was too busy to turn and see what the men in the cab were seeing. He was buckling his turnout coat, pulling on his Nomex hood, cinching the harness straps on his air pack, slipping the lanyard of his face mask around his neck. He saw only what he was doing and, when he looked up in the direction of the hose bed, reflections of their red, white, and blue lights bouncing off the mid-ship control panel. The rookie, in the matching jump seat on the other side of the engine housing, behind their officer, was too nervous and too busy donning his brand new gear to look anywhere or see anything. The Engine Company was on its way to the rookie's first real working fire.

The moment they turned onto Float Street, the driver and his lieutenant could see the house going gang-busters, *rolling* as they said in the firefighting business, burning 'til Hell wouldn't have it, and they were still a block away. The driver stopped the engine just past the corner hydrant. The lieutenant slid the window between himself and the jump seat open. He opened his mouth to speak to the rookie but, beside him, the driver shouted, "Grab it, Rook!" The lieutenant smiled.

The rookie left his seat, moved hurriedly to the back of the engine, grabbed the knuckle of their five-inch supply line (with spanner attached), and lifted it from the bed. He pulled several folds of the line to the pavement, dragged the works to the curb, and wrapped the hydrant. The engine growled and took off, flaking the supply line down the street behind it, headed for the burning house. Left to himself, the eager rookie went to work connecting the line to their water supply.

A lone police officer, who'd spotted the fire and called in the alarm, stood watch before the house. Only a handful of rubber-neckers had gathered, gawking and threatening to get in the way, but it was early (1:30 in the morning) and the fire had only recently shown itself. As the flames grew, as the sirens and lights increased, and the neighbors began to realize what was happening then, despite the iced sidewalks, the freezing air, the winter snow piled everywhere, the scant on-lookers would grow into a crowd. Winter or summer, they always did.

The engine made the curb nearest the house and the engineer climbed down from the cab. He uncoupled his end of the hydrant line, reconnected it to the engine, and climbed amid-ship to ready the pump controls. He passed the veteran firefighter, leaving his jump seat in full turnout gear and air pack, who started down the icy street headed for the rear of the engine. The lieutenant, who didn't like early alarms or the cold, stepped carefully down from his side of the cab to assess the situation. The house was a shabby gray two-story. The downstairs windows, in particular a big picture window looking out onto the front porch, were black with rolling smoke. The window above, probably a bedroom, was black too but intermittently alive with fingers of dancing flame poking through the churn. At the tailboard, the veteran saw it too. "This," he grumbled, "is going to taste like shit."

Firefighting, like any profession, had its routines and the details of fire scene set up aren't necessary. Suffice to say, everything went more or less the way the text book said it should. Engine One arrived with more help and a captain to take command. Ladder One arrived with a couple of meaty, slow-witted truckies to cut roof shingles, pull down ceilings, and break windows. The deputy chief (the city was too small for battalions) showed up in short order with the usual jelly stains on his white uniform shirt. (The chief was home in bed.) More cops showed, of course, to handle traffic, the growing crowd, and to gawk themselves. Two ambulances rounded out the act, not only to treat and cart away the injured but because the paramedics, too, were firefighters. The engineer at the pump controls blew the air horn, two blasts.

Hearing the signal, the rookie cranked open the valve on the fire hydrant and the five-inch supply line filled with water, fat as a honeymoon dick, down the length of the block. Air masks were pulled on, attack lines were charged, and entry was attempted on the burning house.

Attempted was the key word. The front door was sprung but, oddly, wouldn't spring. It just wouldn't open. That's when the feeling started among the firefighters that there was something strange about that house. The front door would have to be chopped out of the frame. With the first attack line stalled there, a second team broke the plate glass living room window, and ate a cloud of black smoke for their trouble. They tried to take the line over the window sill and in and, they too, immediately found their progress arrested. It wasn't unusual for a fire to fight back before it was gotten under control, but that place was kicking their butts before they could get off the porch. Long story short, a hard fought entry was eventually made and the struggle begun to reach the seat of the fire.

Along the way, they discovered the bizarre cause of their troubles. The occupants of the house, it soon became apparent, were hoarders. The whole place, besides being full of smoke and fire, was also full of trash. That's no exaggeration. The floor didn't exist. It was buried by three feet of strewn garbage and collected junk. That was why the front door would not open and why the team coming in through the window could get no further. Blinded in a world of black rolling smoke, they couldn't see they were also surrounded by unending junk. The firefighters could neither crawl, as they often had to, nor could they stand all the way up. The trash upon which they were forced to walk was so high they had to duck to get under doorways. This in the dark, in eighty pounds of turnout gear, dragging hose, breathing bottled air, fighting fire. It was not a good time.

The growing number of gawkers, meanwhile, watching the firemen try to save their neighbors' home were having a great time. Despite the freezing winter night, in their nothing-ever-happens town it was practically a party. A couple of guys even had beer until one of the cops spotted them and ordered the cans dumped. Unhappy in a major key, they argued their rights and called her a bitch to her face. The officer wasn't impressed. She repeated her order and the beer was wasted on the snow.

The rubber-necker having the best time of all was a fellow all alone near the back of the shifting crowd. His name was Doug Gamley and, frankly, he was enjoying the show so much it was all he could do to keep his hand off his pecker. You see, Gamley, and a 'friend' of his (who's yet to officially enter the story), a guy named Kevin Connor, had started the house fire. That's right. On purpose they'd lit it up, in the kitchen and in the living room both, not ten minutes after they'd tied up, and not two or three minutes after they'd killed, the twin brothers who lived there.

The fire took on a bright red-orange thanks to the cold night air. The black smoke chugged out through the new openings, door and window, like nobody's business. Inside, the firefighters couldn't see their gloves in front of their own face masks or, for that matter, find their hind-ends with those same hands. Under those conditions, with the addition of pressurized water that froze in place within minutes of being thrown, it took a good long while for them to 'make bag' as they said in the trade.

In that time, the newest member of the company, the rookie that had seen to the engine's water supply, had left the hydrant and ran the length of the block to get in on the action. Firefighters do not run at fire scenes, for a whole lot of reasons, but he was an eager beaver and that was a lesson he'd yet to learn. Maybe some other day. Now, he wanted to be 'in the shit.' Running was just the first mistake he made in his excitement. He was about to make a whole bunch more. He grabbed an air pack from the ladder truck without telling anyone. He headed into the scene without reporting to Incident Command. And having strapped on an air bottle, and donned his mask, he entered the burning house without any of the other busy firefighters knowing he'd even left the hydrant. He went alone – an absolute no-no – into his very first fire.

The rookie had been through academy so he wasn't surprised it didn't look like fires on television. On TV, unmasked firefighters moved through rooms brightly lit by the fire, shouting heroic dialogue to each other as they rescued the trapped innocents. In the real thing, superheated air and failure to wear the proper equipment meant rapid death. The heat was oppressive, the air filled with rolling black smoke, and you couldn't see a thing. No, he wasn't surprised. But he was quickly disconcerted and lost.

Team two was still in the living room trapped in what amounted to a giant box; its sides made out of furniture (a desk and couch for sure, other items less discernible in the smoke), towering stacked newspapers and books, cardboard boxes of assorted whatsits, and plain, old fashioned garbage (melted two-liter bottles, animal feces, crushed cups, and strangled paper bags featuring a rainbow of famous burger-joint logos). They had to drop their line and, together, shove the desk away and topple one of the paper stacks to free themselves, just so they could climb atop the mound of garbage running through the house and advance the nozzle.

Team one had made it through the front door and down a cluttered hall, reached the kitchen, and found the seat of one of the fires. It was obvious, even with scant details, the house was burning in several places and likely had been started by an arsonist. But that would all be hashed out later. Right now, it was going gang-busters a few feet away and they had to put the damned thing out. Of course, hitting it with water plunged the kitchen back into blackness.

The rookie found his way into the kitchen a moment later; though he had no clue that's what he'd done. He stood in the black rolling smoke only a few feet from the nozzle team – without either being the least aware of the presence of the other. He took a blind and misguided step to his right, through a doorway missing a door, and fell ass-over-tea kettle down a rickety set of wooden stairs. Amid the chaos, the crackling and popping fire, the flying water, splintering wood, shattering glass, the shouts of scrambling firefighters, the squawking radios, and the milling crowd and cops outside, nobody in the kitchen heard a thing out of place. None knew the rookie had ever been there beside them. Or that, now, he was gone again.

The stunned rookie rose to his knees in the basement. He'd knocked his mask askew and couldn't get a breath. He was not only dizzy and beat up, he was suffocating. He rolled off whatever it was that had broken his fall, without being able to see it, and back to his knees. He fought his helmet off, wrestled his mask up and over his head, gasping. Beneath the mask the rookie was a handsome blonde, in his mid-twenties, with a chiseled jaw and soft blue bedroom eyes; eyes that, at that moment, he cast around the cellar.

He could see that it held a good deal of gray smoke filtering down but, as the fire seemed to be all upstairs, none of the rolling black clouds. It also had water, plenty of it, several inches deep on the floor and raining down between the ceiling joists from the activities on the floor above; an indoor shower over a dark stone cage. In spite of the artificial rain, the basement also had an amber glow...

Trying to catch a breath, the gasping, sweating rookie peered through the gloom to the glow. Candles, that's what he was seeing. Lit candles, arranged around a painting on a wall, in what looked to be some sort of shrine. He squinted through the smoke at a star, a five-pointed star, painted within a circle with the candles hung at each point. It was a pentagram, a freaking pentagram just like those seen in the devil, witch, and werewolf movies.

What the heck? Turning back, he closed his eyes and lowered his head to breathe slower, if not easier, to find the best of what air there was near the cellar floor. When he opened them again, he saw what it was he'd landed on, the thing that had broken his fall. It was the body of an old man, dressed in what looked like the black robe of a priest, spattered with blood, sitting upright in the rising water on the floor, his arms behind him, his back against the crumbling limestone wall at the bottom of the stairs. He looked to have taken the same fall the rookie had – with one major difference. The old man had had nothing but the wooden steps and the concrete floor to cushion his fall. And... he had a thick piece of duct tape across his mouth and wrapped around his head.

Panic struck the rookie. Suddenly everything had changed. This was no longer just his first house fire. This was an arson job. This was a murder!

Trembling, he took hold of the old boy and moved him slightly, straining to look behind him. Yes, his hands were tied too. The old man had been gagged, tied up, and pushed down the stairs. The house had been purposely set on fire! Then along came the Fire Department so that he could heroically fall down the same stairs and land on top of the poor old guy. The rookie felt sick to his stomach. He was already breathing like a locomotive, trying to catch his breath in that smoky cellar, now he needed a deeper breath to keep from vomiting. He'd landed right on top of him. But, did it matter, really? The old boy looked deader than dead. He wrestled the tape off the fellow's wrists, brought his thin arms forward and rested his back against the wall. He unwound the tape and yanked it off his mouth. He leaned forward, into his face, listening for breath.

The rookie didn't see the candles on the pentagram flare up behind him. He was too busy crying out in shock as the old man's eyes snapped open.

It scared the living hell out of him, shook him to his core. He would have added a scream to his shout of alarm but he'd yet to get his breath back. He would have sworn on a stack of Bibles the guy was dead. Before the firefighter could recover, the old man's hand shot up from the shallow pool of water building on the floor and clutched him by the throat. His grip was frightening. It pinched like a vice, cutting off his air entirely, preventing even a gasp of terror. And it was terror. The old boy's eyes rolled up and back, leaving nothing but yellowed whites glowing in the deep orbits of his head. His mouth gaped open showing blue gums and missing teeth. A gurgle from the deepest pits of Hell, and a matching stench, escaped his mouth and hit the young fireman full in the face. Then something awful and horrendous passed up and out of the old man's gullet. The rookie jerked hard as whatever it was hit him. He screamed, or would have, but the terrifying swirling essence muted the sound as it punched its way into his mouth and disappeared inside of him. The old man fell back against the wall, dead again. The young firefighter fell back into the water in convulsions.

When the spasm passed and the splashing ebbed, moving stiffly in exaggerated jerks, the rookie sat up. Without a word, he stood. He replaced his black rubber air mask, his face and ferociously staring eyes vanishing behind the thick clouded lens and, over that, donned his carbon coated helmet. He turned to the makeshift altar glowing in the light of the flickering candles. He stared at the pentagram at the center of the dark shrine and, as best he could beneath the air pack and heavy turnout gear, bowed in what looked like a show of deep respect to some dark and invisible authority.

Turning, he splashed across the basement floor, took the rear stone steps up, threw open the wooden doors on the old slanted bulkhead portal, and climbed out of the basement.

The crowd of gawkers, now doubled in size, were having a grand time behind the police barricade. Doug Gamley, still at the back, still relishing the destruction and, in particular, the part he'd played in it, was nevertheless irked that he had to enjoy it alone. Kevin Connor, his bosom buddy, his co-arsonist, had wanted to get the hell away from there as fast as he could. Connor had needed a drink. Connor was a coward who, if you asked Gamley, didn't know where to get the jollies that mattered. Well, Gamley sure did. He didn't need Connor for that. He turned from the Fire Department's excitement to concentrate on his own.

The city boys would have the fire out soon and, once they did, there would be no sense in his hanging around to watch them find the bodies. He scoured the crowd which, even in that dead hour of the morning, in the dead cold of winter, was full to the brim with neighborhood gals he'd sniffed before. Yes, sir, Gamley figured, might as well end the celebration with a warm piece of tail.

So intent was the crowd on the fire, so intent was Gamley on a potential conquest, so intent were the city officials on their duties, nobody saw or paid any mind to a fully suited firefighter that appeared from the shadows at the side of the burning house and circled the crowd. Nobody saw him spot Gamley on the street or paid attention as he maneuvered toward him and stepped behind him. Nobody saw the rookie bring his arm quickly around, jam the fingers of one gloved hand into Gamley's mouth, and yank him backward off his feet.

Gamley tried to scream. But the dirt and carbon embedded in the Nomex was stifling and the thick glove made the slightest noise impossible. He tried to bite the rookie's fingers but found that equally useless. Besides, the firefighter was squeezing him like a bear, squeezing the breath out of him, as he carried him back away from the crowd and around in the direction from which he'd come. With no one any the wiser, Gamley was dragged into the darkness around the side of the house.

One of the required class subjects in fire academy was self-rescue, the art of staying alive in unique emergencies. Being able to escape the upper levels of a structure when you were alone and everything went to shit was high on the list of lessons. As a successful graduate, the rookie carried the necessary personal bailout system in a cargo pocket on one leg of his bunker pants: a rigged rappelling descender, a length of rope, and a Seattle Hook for rapid deployment. The hook was exactly that, seven inches high, five wide, made of polished aluminum with barbed teeth on the inside of the wide purchase point to bite into a parapet wall or railing and hold fast. But the Seattle Hook, they'd been taught, was a multifunctional tool.

There in the shadows, with Gamley pinned against the side of the burning house and going nowhere, the rookie drew the hook from his pocket, turned it in his hand, and smashed it through the murdering arsonist's eye and into his brain. Gamley sputtered noiselessly into his glove, went through a violent spasm, then went limp.

Dragging Gamley's corpse with him, with nobody on the premises aware, the rookie vanished around the corner into the back yard, down the steps, and into the black abyss of the basement.

In the house above, the hose teams were finally making bag. They had extinguished the kitchen and the living room fire was finally being knocked down. The heavy black smoke was turning gray. Front to back, garbage to ceiling, the thousands of gallons of water thrown were freezing, turning the whole shooting match into an alien world of crystal and scorch. A smoke ejector had been hung in the front doorway, getting a small but important start on clearing the air and it looked like C Shift was going to save one. It was then that someone on the first floor, aware of neighborhood scanners and purposely avoiding using his portable, cried out in a voice muffled by his air mask, "We've got a body!"

Unaware of what the rookie had discovered in the basement, ignorant to everything that had transpired behind the crowd outside and directly under their feet since, the firefighters upstairs thought their body was the first. It was buried amid the garbage on the floor, in the shortened archway between the living room and a tiny hall to a ground floor bathroom. In the garbage, it was barely recognizable as a human being, or what had once been a human being. It was burned like a forgotten grill order, black, with the flesh of both legs split like overdone Johnsonville Brats. A closer look showed its arms had been tied behind its back and its mouth taped shut.

Eleven

With one nozzle team still fighting fire, with the laborious work of pulling ceilings and opening walls to chase spot fires and rekindles, and with the added excitement of a victim that had been clearly murdered, the house, the fire scene, and the Command Center were bustling with officials. All of them too busy to notice a lone firefighter, the rookie from Engine Company Two, in full turnout gear, shamble up from the basement, through the shadowed back yard, and away.

Two short residential blocks away, on the next main thoroughfare, sat the Trackside Bar and Grill. It was a seedy little drinking joint with seedier customers slouched over heavy wooden tables covered in just the right number of stains. Fewer and they'd have wanted livelier customers. More and they would have had no customers at all. The titled 'Bar' was self-evident. The titled 'Grill' was forgettable; everyone in the know ate before arriving. As for the 'Trackside' part, it bore that moniker not because there was a race track within a hundred miles, but because there was an OTB across the street.

Sitting in a corner at one of the tables was the other, unofficial, reason for the establishment's name, the local bookmaker, Kevin Connor, Doug Gamley's partner in arson. With Connor sat his girlfriend, a barfly he affectionately called 'the Dirty Blonde'. She was chugging beer from a bottle. Connor hated the taste of beer. It was booze for him, gin if he could get it – neat, no ice, no soda, no twist. But there was nothing neat about the way he drank it. He threw it back, as his red eyes and blossomed nose proved, especially when he wasn't happy. And Connor was not happy.

"Was his own fault," Connor muttered to the Dirty Blonde. "His own damned fault. I got a right to my money. What's he doing betting if he can't afford to lose? Nobody should bet if they can't afford to lose. Bill Seaton wasn't no good; couldn't tell a horse from a greyhound. Didn't know one ball team from another. Just a stupid old man that had to bet. The big win was always just around the corner. But he was a loser and he wouldn't pay up. Was his own damned fault."

"What, honey?" the Dirty Blonde asked, not listening.

Connor swallowed gin. "I just wanted my money. And Bill wouldn't pay. Ain't bad enough I gotta track him down. He lives like a pig, surrounded by garbage and dead animals. You looked around; there was a pile of trash, a mountain of old newspapers, a mound of dried dog shit, then some wet dog shit, then a dead dog all in a row like they belonged there in the house. So Bill Seaton won't pay. Then here comes Bill's twin brother, Rosie, like the world needed two of those creeps. But the brother is fucking creepier. He comes up out of the basement like some kind of ghoul, wearing a long black robe, waving his hands in our faces, and saying Bill ain't got to pay. Screaming that the devil protects them both. Can you believe that crap?"

"The devil?" the Dirty Blonde asked.

"S'what the prick said. He could have gone somewhere while we did business with Bill. Or minded his own business and not stuck his nose in. But, no, he's standing there like some kind of evil priest and tells us to get out or Satan will have his revenge on us. What the hell?"

"So what'd you do?"

"I didn't do nothing. I didn't get a chance. I got Gamley there for muscle. Gamley's got a temper and – boom – he slapped the shit out of the old warlock. Slapped him right down to the floor beside his brother. Would have slapped him to death... But then he gets an idea."

"Doug Gamley? An idea?"

"Yeah, s'what I said. Gamley grabs a roll of duct tape and takes a coupla' laps around each of their mugs to shut 'em up. Tapes their hands behind their backs; ties 'em up like they're Christmas geese. Then he yanks old Bill up by the few hairs left on his head and tells him he's gonna pay his book tab or, Gamley said, he's gonna watch him punch his creepy brother's ticket."

"Punch his ticket?"

"Kill him, you dumb broad."

"Who you calling dumb?"

"Am I talking to you?"

"I don't know," she said, chewing the lipstick off her bottom lip. "It's me or yourself. So, you tell me, who you talking to?"

"I'm not talking to. I'm talking about. And you're interrupting." Connor gulped gin. "Bill, the dumb ass, says he'd pay if he could, but whines that he just can't. So what's Gamley do? Lifts Rosie up like he's a bag of trash, looks him right in the beady eyes and says, 'Sorry asshole, your brother won't pay his bill, so you get to pay it for him.' Then he turned to the basement, told Rosie, 'Say Hi to Satan, jerk-off,' and chucked him down the basement stairs right on his head.

"My God! He could of killed him!"

"Stifle it!" Connor shouted in a whisper. "He did kill him! What do you think?" Connor stared into his empty glass while he shook with the memory. "I thought he was kidding. So did Bill, I guess. We was both wrong. Gamley killed Rosie's witch ass without blinking. Now Bill's screaming like a bitch under the duct tape. But it's too late. By then, Gamley's got a taste for blood and he's gone, mental, you know. Suddenly he's shaking his head like his McDonald's drive-through order was screwed up. And he turned to Bill with blood in his eyes and said, 'Wasn't enough. Your brother wasn't worth a damn, so you still owe.' I tried to stop him. I said, 'Hey, man. . .' But there wasn't no stopping him. He didn't even hear me. Two minutes later, Bill was deader than hell. I'm yelling at him that I ain't gonna get my money. And Gamley is yelling that it's their own damn fault and I oughtta shut up."

Connor took a breath. "I told him, thanks to him, I was out the money for good. And he said I'd be out a lot more if I didn't help him."

"Help him what?"

"The place is on fire, ain't it? It went up like dried hay. He said we had to get rid of the evidence, so we burned it. I didn't want Bill dead. I had no complaint with his twin. Hell, his creepy brother wasn't even supposed to be there. But Rosie Seaton started shooting his mouth off, promising hexes, and curses, and all the demons of Hell. Fucking weirdo! Both of 'em. It's their own damned fault."

"I know honey," the blonde said, patting his hand. "I hear ya."

"You don't know nothing, understand?" Conner barked with a mean glint in his eyes. "You didn't hear a word of this! You don't know a damned thing, get me?"

Guided, apparently, by whatever powers the late Rosie Seaton possessed, and with the two blocks behind him, the rookie moved into the shadows at the rear of the Trackside Bar and Grill. He tilted his helmeted head, stared through the dark shield of the face piece, and caught sight of the stretch of electrical wires from the top of the pole at the mouth of the alley to the weather head at the service entrance on the Bar's roof. He followed the conduit down to the meter base and watched the small tin wheel spin. Around his waist the rookie wore a thick leather truck belt with dangling firefighting equipment: a spanner wrench, a heavy duty flashlight (superfluous now, as he could see in the dark), and a keenly sharpened hand ax. This last, the rookie pulled from his belt. He drew back, swung, and brought it down hard across the electric meter. Sparks flew.

Inside, the bar was plunged into darkness. The music and lights died together while the crowd came alive in an uproar. It seemed about even; half the customers barked drunken complaints to the other half's drunken laughter. The bartender grumbled his way into the kitchen and started flipping breakers in the electric panel. He got nothing. Aware of his shortcomings as an electrician, he decided to thank his lucky stars and call it a night. All the bitching in the world didn't matter after that. He was closing.

The bartender told his customers so. He blamed the city, the electric company, and the house fire a few streets down for putting the matter out of his hands. He told everybody to drink up then rode that old horse once around the bar, "You don't have to go home, but you can't stay here."

From the shadows of the back alley, the rookie watched the patrons, alone and in groups, abandon the dark bar. He moved closer into the black triangle of shadow beside the door to watch the Dirty Blonde barfly strike out; first with Connor, who wasn't in the mood, then with two other guys in quick succession. With nothing to look forward to but a dry, lonely night, she stepped outside alone. Unaware of the rookie in the shadows behind her, the Dirty Blonde stumbled down the front steps and wobbled away on heels that looked and probably felt much higher than they had at the start of the evening.

The sneering Connor was the last to leave. He stepped out growling, mad as hell at being forced out, and kept howling his discontent as the bar keep closed and locked the door in his face. Grumbling, he left the shadowed doorway. He rounded the corner of the bar and started down the alley. He'd gone only a few paces when Connor must have realized he was headed back to the burning house. He pulled up, examined the situation, came to whatever conclusion he came to and, waving it away, turned on his heels. He immediately stopped again.

The rookie was there, in full yellow, carbon-covered regalia: boots, pants, coat, air pack, face mask, and wide helmet; a lost firefighter blocking his way. Connor blinked his bleary unbelieving eyes. He shook his head and blinked again. The only sound in the otherwise silent night was the heavy measured breathing inside the firefighter's mask. Connor belched. "What... the... hell?"

The rookie snatched Connor by the throat. He jerked the inebriated arsonist off his feet before his gin fogged mind could comprehend what was happening. He retreated with him deeper into the dark alley behind the building. He drew the ax from his belt again and slowly, relishing the moment, lifted it above his helmet. Connor's eyes grew wide as moonlight touched the oiled blade.

"Who... are you?" Connor croaked in a strangled whisper. He couldn't get a breath. He didn't get a response. Connor panicked. He flailed his arms striking the rookie in the chest and head. Between the thick material, the harness, the helmet, and his own booze-sapped strength, he might just as well have been spitting in the wind. The firefighter tightened his grip.

"Who... are... you?" Connor's eyes began to drift as he lost focus and his consciousness slipped away. Still, the bookmaker made one final terrified attempt, lashing out with his last ounce of strength. His thumb hooked the air hose at the front of the fireman's face piece. His panicked jerk knocked the rookie's helmet to the ground and brought the mask up and over his head. The air mask, hanging from a strap about the firefighter's neck, swung like a pendulum at his chest. Connor's eyes followed the strap up – and he gasped.

The rookie, the handsome blond with chiseled jaw and bedroom eyes, was gone. What the arsonist saw was the old man, the dead Rosie Seaton, bound and burned two blocks away in the house on Float Street, grinning at him. Rosie laughed. Then his head burst into flames. The flesh twisted and his features bubbled in the raging heat. He laughed on and was soon joined by the laughter of a chorus of demons from Hell. Connor screamed.

The rookie brought the ax down with a *thwack*.

When the twitching ended, the rookie retrieved his ax from Connor's broken melon, wiped the sticky juices on the bookmaker's pants, and slipped the tool back into his truck belt. He donned his face piece and helmet again. He lifted Connor's worthless carcass onto his shoulder and carried it the two deserted blocks back to the fire scene. With the crowd yet distracted out front, he carried the body through the back yard, unnoticed, and threw it through the cellar doors into the basement. He followed it in.

Into the man-made pool – that's what the basement had become with the water from the floors above now a torrential rain. Three of the five candles on the black altar had been extinguished by the deluge, while the remaining two managed the merest amber nimbus in the gray smoke. Gamley's body lay atop a rickety wooden table before the altar.

The rookie grabbed Connor's corpse by the collar and splashing his way, dragged it through the two foot-deep water, lifted it dripping, and laid it atop the other. The table creaked with the weight. The rookie splashed to a rack of shelves in the corner, picked out a can of gasoline from among the items stored there, and poured the contents (three gallons, give or take) over the pair. Taking one of the two remaining lit candles from the altar, with a repeat of the respectful bow, he set the corpses on fire.

The flames only just reached the ceiling joists when there came an ominous rumble. The first floor, beneath the weight of the kitchen appliances, uncounted years of collected trash, uncounted gallons of freshly thrown water, and several tons of ice collapsed atop the demonic funeral pyre as part of the first floor fell into the basement. Smoldering wood, plaster, linoleum, paper, metal, water, and ice rained down, burying the rookie, the burning sacrifice, and the black altar.

As the debris-filled indoor pool settled, there followed excited shouting from above. The shouts soon drew near the cellar stairs. A relatively clean and pressed lieutenant looked down from above while a band of his firefighters descended. One of them spotted a carbon covered yellow plastic fire helmet floating in the pool. "Geez, look at that!" He jumped in, grabbed the helmet, lifted it, and brought the rookie up with it. He pitched the helmet forward and off. He grabbed the face piece by the air hose and pulled the mask up and back. He stared down into the gasping face of the blond, square-jawed firefighter. "You all right, Rook?"

In answer, the exhausted rookie turned and vomited into the basement pool.

"I can't say I blame you, kid," the veteran said. "It's been a hell of a night."

With tearing eyes, the rookie looked past his brother firefighters, through the smoke, dust, and flying embers, to the scorched wall drawing, illuminated now by a lone candle, running and barely recognizable anymore as a pentagram. The rookie could only nod his head in bewildered silence.

"But it's good experience," his colleague continued. "There's a lot of damned evil in this world. And you never know who or what's standing right beside you."

Twelve

Herb Flay pounded the hub cab back into place with a tinny *bang, bang, bang* that almost – almost – made music with the rain. The job was done, the tire changed, and the middle knuckle on his right hand had stopped throbbing and appeared to have stopped bleeding. Sometime over the last twenty minutes, he wasn't sure when, while shifting the gurney and equipment about the rear compartment to get at the jack and spare tire, in getting the van raised on the jack, in getting the ruined tire off, or in getting the spare secured in its place, Flay had torn his knuckle. He had no memory of injuring himself, but there he was bleeding like a stuck pig. Marlowe would be short one towel at the scene.

Speaking of Marlowe and busted knuckles... When rolling a casket on a church truck (the wheeled cart beneath the casket that nobody ever sees; and never 'coffin', by the way, always 'casket') to and from the hearse, in or out of the funeral home or church, Marlowe would throw a fit if he saw any of his workers pushing or pulling said casket by any of the attached handles. Two people moved a casket, on a church truck, and did so with their hands firmly gripping – and protecting – the top corners of each end. The hands were the bumpers as the casket passed through a door frame or by anything immovable. "Your knuckles, *ehh*, will heal. The casket won't!" Maybe that's why Flay didn't notice the injury he'd done himself at first. His knuckles were used to it.

Tire on, he jacked the van back to the ground, *terra infirma* with the downpour, stored the tools back away, made what order he could again of the gurney and equipment, to appease what by now would be an anxious and agitated Marlowe, and prayed he could coax the van back up onto the road.

A bright spot, if you could call it that, on that dark and stormy night, was that Flay no longer needed the address of the house that Marlowe had scribbled out for him. Though he was still more than a block away from his destination, *it* had reached him, across the distance through the rain; that monstrous, ungodly odor. Reached him, please! It had enveloped him like a shroud. It wasn't merely death; he'd smelled death. (He'd only been there for four months, but Fengriffin's was not the first funeral home for which Flay had worked.) It was an explosion of the smells created by the tornado of activity inside a decaying corpse. No, Flay no longer needed the address. The sickening smell would lead the way.

The laughter inside the Proprietor's garage had died. Henderson's story had killed it, embalmed it, and laid it to rest. The story of the demon possessed firefighter, among that group of already edgy civil servants, had struck just a little too close to home. Now there really was a sense of evil in the thick air.

It was the perfect moment, thought the old coroner, who lived, loved, and laughed by his gallows humor, to drive another – perhaps a final – nail in the coffin. And, yes, the word that occurred to him was 'coffin'. Why ruin a good cliché just because Marlowe was a tight-ass? The coroner doffed his spectacles and polished the lenses with a worn white hanky, muttering, "No doubt about it, Paul, that was a gooder. Yes, sir, that story was... What do the kids say today? A freaker! But was it true?"

Henderson shrugged and sipped his coffee.

"Because I'll tell you one," the coroner said, "that's true." He nodded, letting a memory flood back. "*Everything* about that case was strange. But it was also true. The cops, no offense to our sheriff here, had plenty of clues, but no clue how the puzzle went together." The coroner returned his glasses to their place, working the temple tips around the tops of his ears. "The fella's name was Soames. He was a hospital security guard. Casc like that you never forget. John Soames."

The coroner shook his head. "I'd trade a piece of my retirement to know, for sure, what in the world happened that night."

Thirteen

Out of frustration and, frankly, for the pure hell of it, John Soames stomped the brakes, fish-tailing his security vehicle across the icy drive. It came to a stop against a drift facing the opposite direction. *Good enough*, he thought, throwing the transmission into *Park*. For these people, it was good enough. He kept the motor running for the heater, what little there was of it, rubbed the frost from the side window, and stared up through the gloom at the original, now abandoned, hospital.

He shook his head in dismay. "What a load of crap."

What had Francis called the place? Or was it Fred? Soames wasn't good with names, especially first names, and that joker's first and last were both first names. Security supervisor Fred Francis; that was it. *Whoopee.* The guy was an idiot, treated him with no respect whatsoever. And talk about green. Soames had kids older than his new supervisor. (And they didn't treat him with any respect either.) What the hell, it was a job. He'd needed the job; needed the money. That is, if you could call the pittance the hospital offered for night-shift security work *money*. It wasn't right; for a guy with his experience. But those were the times. You had to roll with the times. He'd feel better when he got his first check. Wouldn't he? Speaking of which, Soames thought, he'd better go pretend to earn it.

He zipped his coat, pulled on his hat and gloves. Knowing he'd be right back, he left the motor run. He mumbled, "Let's get this nonsense over with," then, dreading the arctic blast, forced himself out of the car. The chill bit instantly. He shivered and exhaled a frosty cloud. Cold, dead winter and he'd been sent to the back of the property, the end of nowhere, on patrol. Fifty-three years old, eighteen degrees Fahrenheit, and he was shaking forgotten doors. Why him, for God's sake? No reason, other than that he was the *new* man. Disrespectful bastards, that's what his bosses were.

He looked to the south to the gleaming white skyline of buildings communally known as Mercy General, the sprawling new hospital for which he now labored, glowing in the night. He turned back, staring up at the original facility from which all else had sprung, now just a blot on the back-forty; a long-abandoned, unlit five-story rectangle of ancient red brick and crumbling mortar almost black against the gray night sky with rows of dirty and broken windows sightlessly looking out like empty orbits in an old skull.

"It's haunted." That's what Francis had said, calmly, point-blank, as if it were just a fact he was passing on. "Haunted?" Soames had studied the face of his young, too serious to be taken seriously, boss looking for a smirk. None appeared. Still it was clear the guy was putting him on and Soames didn't bother to hide it that he knew. "Nonsense." It wasn't a word he normally used, too sedate. But hollering 'Bullshit!' at your boss on your first night didn't seem the thing to do. "Pure nonsense!"

"With deference to your experience, Officer Soames, you don't know what you're laughing at. You may have seen plenty, but you're new here." With that, Francis went on with his in-service, feeding him one slice of bent history after another about the hospital, its grounds, and this dilapidated dump as if it was all perfectly natural. That, Soames thought, had been disrespectful too; treating him like a kid around a campfire. His training, as far as this place was concerned, had been nothing but a ghost story.

Built in 18-'something-or-other' (Soames was no good with dates either), the place was already weather-beaten and losing bricks when the doctors and nurses were treating ball shots, bayonet wounds, and typhus in the War Between the States. She wasn't Mercy General then. Why a hospital was called *she*, Soames didn't know, but back then she was the gentler, hope-filled Our Lady of Mercy. Like the luckier soldiers, she survived the Civil War. The building, originally three-stories and square (he'd been shown an old brown picture), rose up, grew out, and overtook the neighboring properties: a blacksmith and livery stable, a saloon, a general store, so Francis had said. As the town grew the hospital grew with it. The locals called her simply *Lady Mercy*. The century turned, the decades passed and, within her walls, the joys and horrors of human existence passed too: birth, death, and every imaginable injury and illness in-between. Lives were saved, diseases fought, plagues suffered. Laughter, groans of despair, screams of agony echoed from her ceilings and passed in waves through her windows. Limbs were amputated. Cures were found. Souls were lost.

Soames stared up at the disused tomb. He clapped his gloves and stomped his boots feeling the cold. He felt the dark as well with a different chill no stomping could lessen. The only remedy was to finish the patrol. He started into the snow (maintenance had no reason to shovel there). He shook the south, once upon a time the front, doors and found them secure. He started around the looming edifice, the wreck of Lady Mercy. He saw nothing but the abandoned hospital and the snow. He heard nothing but the wind. He felt nothing but the cold. As Soames trudged on his mind had little to do but wander. And, inspired by the setting, where could it roam but over the details of Francis' ghost story.

The nurses, orderlies, and housekeepers who kept the old hospital running in the Deathwatch hours, began to hear odd sounds, to smell strange odors, to see unbelievable sights in the night. Rumor had it that several nurses, one or two children, and a handful of soldiers that had passed away within its walls during that bloody Civil War had failed to pass on to their afterlife. The place developed an odd, at first, and then a frightening reputation that slowly spread in whispered warnings. Meanwhile, a clinic annex was built in the distance. Staff members were, not surprisingly, grateful to be transferred to the new facility. The original hospital saw less and less use. By the staff, that is. Ridiculous as it was, stories persisted of more frequent use by the spirits of the dead. Eventually, as in life, where the daughter becomes the mother, the son the father, the annex became the hospital and was rechristened Mercy General. The name, Our Lady of Mercy, was relegated to history and the original hospital relegated to office space and dormitory use. One might have thought that the end of the mysterious troubles but it was in fact only the beginning. The strange occurrences increased until the building's residents could stand no more. The nursing program was ended and the X-ray techs moved to a new dorm. Mercy General prospered while Lady Mercy was reduced to storage space. The haunting... Soames shook his head recalling it, but that was the word Francis used. The haunting continued and, when the maintenance crews would no longer enter without complaint, the building was abandoned.

Even death was not the end. With no budget for repairs, decay took over. Decay was a new form of life. Vermin laid claim to the basement and halls, graffiti the walls, and the windows surrendered to rocks and to rain, and the old hospital stood alone decomposing for the world to see. Lady Mercy was eventually ordered demolished to make way for new construction. But increased sightings and inexplicable sounds, weird lights and spectral figures, odd accidents and, finally, the death of a demolition worker postponed, then canceled, those plans. From then on, every new group of hospital managers, in their turn, considered knocking the building down and each, for unspoken reasons, gave up on the idea. Whatever existed within the walls of the old hospital had, apparently, won. She would stand until she fell of her own accord. Those outside, who still had the courage to speak her name, changed it again unofficially, and said it now in a whisper, "*No Mercy.*" The century turned again and the stories became legend; something inside that dead relic lived on.

The snow crunched quicker now beneath Soames' feet agitated as he was by the memory of his supervisor's story. The frozen clouds of his exhaled breath came quicker and louder. Still he would have denied his surroundings were bothering him. There were no such things as ghosts! That was exactly what he'd told Francis. "Believe what you will," his boss replied. "I've seen them. I'm telling you, No Mercy is ruled by phantoms. While you're working here you'll respect their wishes." Respect their wishes! He'd never heard such a load of crap. It was just an empty building.

Then again, Soames thought, maybe he and the ghosts would get along fine. Didn't he and the hospital have a lot in common? After years of loyal service hadn't his former employers abandoned him? Hadn't the wife, to who he'd devoted fifteen insufferable years, done the same? What was he but haunted; a wanderer in search of his soul? And where was he? Freezing his butt off in the middle of the night, that's where; under orders to respect a ruined building containing nothing but bat shit and faded memories of war. The ghosts could get in line. Where the hell was his respect? Tramping through the heavy snow toward the back entrance on the north side, Soames slipped and went down. He struggled back to his feet, shouting and sharing his curses with the heavens, and the upper floors of the building. He fell silent, frozen as deadly still as the world around him. A shadow had just appeared in one of the windows.

He stared, neither blinking nor breathing. Yes, he saw something, someone... He forced a breath. "One, two, three, four," he whispered aloud. The shadow moved slightly at the edge of a window on the... fifth floor, near the middle of the building. As he stared, Soames' idiotic conversation with Francis returned again and rang in his ears.

"The troubled spirits of Lady Mercy don't want to be bothered. Just secure the perimeter. Leave the building alone."

"How can you secure it if you don't walk the halls?"

"They walk the halls."

"They? Who are they?"

"Does it matter? Look, Soames, I'm not going to pull my punches because you're older than me. I was once like you; I knew everything. Then I discovered it's what you learn after you know it all that matters." Francis attitude changed as he began what sounded like a confession. "The night I assumed this job, despite the warnings I'd received, and no doubt because I knew it all, I made the men patrol inside Lady Mercy." He hesitated (too dramatically for Soames' tastes). "I can't explain what happened. Just know that we began to hear things and see things... and feel things... and fear things. To be honest, we were chased out. Call it what you like, but we left with an understanding."

"Which was?"

"Did you ever read Shirley Jackson?"

"Not much of a reader; the sports page and the obits. Why? Who's she?"

"Never mind; just believe me, whatever walks in No Mercy wants to walk alone. Stay out of the building. Make sure it's secure and leave *them* be. They don't want us there. Respect their wishes."

It had been a hell of a conversation between two grown men. Now there he was up to his knees in snow, alone outside of the supposedly empty No Mercy, seeing a figure in a window. "Cripes!" He looked about, cold as death and chilled by paranoia, for a hidden camera (or hidden supervisor) tucked away in a drift of snow, watching. Was this all some kind of rookie test? Soames grunted. He was new to the company, not to the world; he wasn't born yesterday. He looked up again to see the figure move away from the window back into the room.

Two could play, Soames thought, pulling his radio from its holster. He'd toss the ball back into Francis' court. "Unit Two to Unit One." He repeated the call, several times over several long cold minutes, but got no reply; nothing but static. So the boss wouldn't take the hand-off. More disrespect.

It didn't matter. Nor did it matter whether the trespasser above was a test or not. He'd been hired to see the facility was secure, hadn't he? Clearly it was not. The tales of hearing and smelling Civil War ghost farts made no difference now. Somebody was inside. Screw Mr. Wet-behind-the-ears Francis and his hospital on haunted hill. He had a job to do.

Soames pulled his key ring from his belt, hoping the neglected lock wouldn't give him trouble. On the contrary, and to his alarm, the building wasn't locked! The hinges complained miserably as the door came open and he stared through a curtain of spiders' webs into the gloom. Soames decided then and there not only to enter but to make an entrance. He took a breath of cold air, slapped a hole in the sticky web, and stepped through, shouting, "All right. Listen up, folks. There's a new sheriff in town!"

He pulled the door closed behind, held his breath, and heard his echo die. He stepped into what decades before had been the foyer, and paused for a new sound that reached his ears – low and hollow moan that added icing to his already chilled spine. "Knock it off," he told himself. Of course, it wasn't a moan at all but the wind calling through a broken window. He thought of a curse for the weather, for Francis and his stupid ghost story, for himself for being so gullible. Ten steps in and his nerves were already a-jangle. He entered the wide receiving area, switched on his Kel-lite, and passed it around to see the room was no longer receiving anybody. Institutionalized emptiness, Soames felt it. He felt as alone and abandoned as the building.

But he knew he wasn't. He'd seen something, someone, in a window above. He was being paid to secure this dung-heap and that's what he was going to do. No electricity meant no lights, no heat and, of course, no elevator. He followed the hall to the end, through atmospheric debris and clutter at his feet and light fixtures dangling on wires about his ears, to a long-unused staircase and started up.

Fourteen

Oddly, within seconds, the stairwell seemed warm and impossibly heated. By the time he reached the second floor landing, Soames had pulled off his hat and gloves and tucked them in his pockets. Who knew, maybe, like everyone else, winter was afraid to enter? The rats were not. He could hear them squeaking and scratching, along with *God-knew-what-else* skittering in the dark. The stairs creaked beneath his feet, the wind continued to moan, the frozen old building to pop and to groan. It all made for inspiring background music.

He was sweating by the time he reached the third floor. Feeling desperately out of shape, he unzipped his coat to cool off. By the fourth floor landing, he found he was just plain hot and had to pause to catch his breath. Whatever ghosts were in residence, he mused, must have been visiting from the tropics. Absentmindedly, Soames pulled off his coat and let it fall to the floor. His throat went dry and his pulse grew rapid. Though he was breathing harder, he noted with some confusion that his frozen breath had vanished. He made an effort to calm himself and started up again.

Soames arrived on the top floor landing a shaken man. Sweating profusely, less winded by the climb than by the climate, he paused again to catch his breath – and to curse Francis for putting crazy thoughts into his head. Ghosts! Not just haunting the place but claiming ownership, demanding respect. What a load of horseshit. He thought again of whoever it was he'd seen at the window, then pictured himself laying his flashlight upside their skull. How about that for a laugh and a lesson, Francis?

A window set in the wall looked in on the fifth floor hallway, or would have had it not been thick with dust. With nothing to clean the glass but his sleeve, Soames skipped it. He'd do without the peek. He opened the stairwell door, stepped into the dark hall, and called out, "Security on the floor." He wasn't a cop, wasn't interested in sneaking up to make a bust. He wanted whoever was there to hear him and get out. "Security on the floor!" The echo hung on the stale air. He carved the darkness down the musty hall with his light. A dozen doors, closed and open, lined either side into the depths. Around them and across the ceiling, black splotches of mold and spiders' webs fought for dominion over the peeling gray paint.

Tough as he was, Soames had to admit he was on edge. The inexplicable stairwell heat had followed him onto the floor. He was burning up. He was burning inside too, just thinking of how he was being treated on his first night. If Francis and the shadowy figure he'd hired for this prank, or his ghosts for that matter, really could read minds, they weren't going to feel very damned respected when they gave his brain a gander. There'd been no answer to his radio call and he'd had no choice but to enter the building.

There'd been no reply to his arrival on the floor and that was fine by him too. He hadn't stopped below and he wouldn't stop now. If the trespasser wouldn't come out, Soames would go find him. He started forward, three steps with three resounding echoes...

A light shot suddenly out of the dark, burst in brilliant fluctuations of orange, yellow, and bleeding red, and overwhelmed the hall. Already suffocated by the heat, now blinded by the light and dizzy with vertigo, Soames fell screaming. He hit the hallway floor hard on his hands and knees, feeling as if he'd been tossed into a raging fire, as if he'd fallen into Hell, and all he could do was pinch his eyes closed against the diabolical glare.

As if his senses were not already overwhelmed, from nowhere, yet clearly from very nearby, the sonorous voice of a pipe organ intruded and began to play. A disbelieving Soames cried out again. But he was hearing it; haunting old organ music. What the hell? Rather than frighten him, it infuriated and embarrassed Soames. He grabbed hold of the wall and, still squinting against the light, pushed himself to his feet. He was being made a fool of. The haunted hospital. "My ass!" Soames screamed. It was like the title of a bad movie or worse, a graphic novel. The orange light continued to flare, the organ played on, but Soames was determined now to ignore it, to find the source of both and lay down the law.

But it was not going to be easy for now the tempo of the music began to march and as if things weren't crazy enough, a rousing chorus began to sing.

Tramp, tramp, tramp, the boys are marching,
Cheer up comrades they will come,
And beneath the starry flag
We shall breathe the air again,
Of the free land in our own beloved home.

Soames shook his head as he realized that the music was coming from the first room on his left. He gritted his teeth, grabbed the old glass door knob as if he was strangling it, and burst through. There was nobody and nothing but an unfurnished room lit by the fingers of orange light reaching round him and, from the opposite side, by gloomy winter moonlight stealing in through a dirty window.

The organ was still playing... behind him now. Swallowing hard, clenching his fists to stifle a tremor, Soames turned and stepped back into the hall. Though just as loud, the tempo of the music had eased and a sullen bass voice had started to sing:

In the prison cell I sit,
Thinking Mother dear, of you,

Clearly, and no mistaking it this time, the solo was coming from the next room down on the opposite side of the hall.

And our bright and happy home so far away,

With the sweat running in streams down his temples, licking his dry lips, Soames pushed the door open. Again, there was nothing but a vacant room – this one with its window broken.

*And the tears they fill my eyes
Spite of all that I can do,
Tho' I try to cheer my comrades and be gay.*

The organ continued to play, behind him again, thundering as it regained its tempo. Soames returned to the hall with his heartbeat and breathing doing the same. The chorus was shouting now:

*Tramp, tramp, tramp, the boys are marching,
Cheer up comrades they will come,*

"Stop it!" Soames screamed.

*And beneath the starry flag
We shall breathe the air again,*

He threw his hands to his ears and pinched his eyes shut. "Stop it! God damn you!"

Of the free land in our own beloved home.

The light disappeared; with it went the music and the heat. The phantom chorus vanished with barely an echo. All were replaced by gray gloom and the lonely whistle of a chill wind as winter overwhelmed the tattered hallway. Soames stood panting in the cold and in terror as blinded by the dark as he had been by the light. His breath came again in great clouds and he hugged himself for warmth. The sweat froze on his face and neck and it suddenly dawned on him, fool that he was, he'd discarded his coat in the dead of winter!

He turned back to retrieve it but found the stairwell door locked. "Damn it." He examined it, found there was no lock, and gawped in confusion. He wrestled with the handle, straining until the cold made his fingers ache from the effort. Still it wouldn't turn and the door would not open. "God damn it!"

Soames considered the window in the wall, now looking out over the stairs, and decided he had no choice but to break it. First day on the job or not, he'd break it, get the hell out of there, and face the consequences later. To check the landing was clear, he laid a forearm on the glass, sacrificing the clean shirt sleeve, and scrubbed a swath through the dirt. A face stared back from the other side.

Soames screamed and fell back. He landed with a thud against the wall but jerked his head up, locking his eyes on the grimy window and, in horror, on the young man on the other side staring at him. He was little more than a boy dressed as a soldier; a Confederate soldier! He had wet, blue eyes sunk in a sickly face as ash-gray as his worn uniform. He moved his lips without making a sound and clutched a faded yellow rag to his throat. Blood streamed between his fingers, down over his hand, and into his sleeve. Soames blinked – and the boy disappeared.

The panicked guard scrambled to his feet, pressed his face against the glass, and studied the landing. There was nothing, nothing but the gloom. A building anger fought for control of his mind, pushed away the fear, insisting he hadn't seen what he'd seen. There were no such things as ghosts! Someone was screwing with him, that was all; screwing with the new guy. They'd fed him a plate of bull about ghosts wanting to be left alone and demanding their respect. They'd come at him with actors and lights to make him swallow it. That was it!

"Respect this!" Soames shouted. He shook a finger in the air as his voice echoed down the hall. "Respect this, Freddie!" Yes, it was childish, but he felt better. With the rage came the realization he wasn't feeling the cold as much. Forget the coat. He wouldn't give them the satisfaction of seeing him break the window to get it.

He laughed instead to show his contempt. "Okay, Casper," he shouted. "You won that round. You're a ghost and you got my coat." He thumbed his chest. "But I'm still wearing the badge!" He started down the hall, picking up his pace, headed for the south exit, but telling himself he would finish the patrol en route. There was, after all, somebody still in the building. He'd seen him; a kid hired by Francis, wearing a costume, with a butt Soames could kick.

As if his violent thought was a stage cue, a gust of wind exploded from the far end of the hall and raced toward him like an angry child. In its wake, with the fury of a dozen cannons fired in succession, every closed door along the way flew open, and every opened door slammed shut. The hall shuddered and Soames screamed.

When the echo died the silence was all-consuming. Stunned and windblown, Soames fought to catch a breath, panting again in great frozen clouds. He'd had enough. He needed to leave. He hurried down the hall, eyeballing the open rooms as he went but not daring to touch the doors that were closed. Near the end of the hall, he stopped as an impossible new sound reached his ears – running water.

He knew from the in-service that the water, like the electricity, had been shut off ages ago; that with hydrants nearby the building had been disconnected from the city mains. Still, just outside of a door marked by a dirty tin plate reading Lavatory, Soames clearly heard water running inside. "What the hell?" he said under his breath. He cracked the door to be certain, heard water running from a tap, and croaked, "Security." There was no response. The water ran on. He rapped the door, quick and loud not to be ignored. "Security." No response. "Francis? Whoever! Identify yourself."

He peered in. The room was small with faded green paper peeling from the walls. The plumbing dated to the middle of the last century with two wooden commode stalls that were missing doors along the left wall, two porcelain sinks on the right behind the door and, on the far end, a wide stall of the same faded wood, this one with a door, protecting an old bathtub. He pushed in. The sinks were rust-stained, filled with dust and broken tiles, and dry as a bone. The commodes were dry too, used only by spiders. There wasn't a soul in sight. Yet in that empty bathroom, in that building with no running water, Soames clearly heard water running. He heard it still before him. Someone was using the bathtub.

"Security," he told the stall. "You're trespassing. If you need..." He shivered involuntarily, unable to imagine taking a tub in this... "If you need to dress, say so, and I'll wait outside the door." In answer, the running water ceased. For a moment it was quiet as the grave. Then a new sound came – splashing. Someone was splashing water in the tub.

Soames rapped angrily on the stall. "Come out of there!" The playful splashing continued. He pushed on the door and, of course, found it locked. Great! Just what he wanted to do, crawl under on that dirty floor to drag some wet scumbag out of the tub. He peered through the gap at the edge of the door – and sucked in a bushel of air. The tub was as dry as a desert and coated in dust. He continued to stare, still clearly hearing water splash, as the hairs stood on the back of his neck. Someone, something unseen, was bathing in front of him in an empty tub! "My God," Soames whispered.

The splashing stopped and a shrill scream erupted from the stall. Soames' blood froze. His spine turned to jelly. Behind him, the bathroom door burst open as if kicked and stood open as if it were being held. But the frame was empty. From the vacant doorway came a shout of rage, then something hit Soames hard in the chest. It drove him back through the splintering stall door and into the tub.

Fifteen

"John Soames went missing for hours," the coroner told the gathered. "His radio had died; he couldn't be reached. His supervisor, Fred Francis, found him at dawn the next morning, at the scene of the long defunct Our Lady of Mercy Hospital, as dead as his radio, sitting upright behind the steering wheel of his security vehicle. The ignition was still on, but the car had run out of gas. Soames was soaking wet from the top of his head to the soles of his squishy Oxfords and, despite being completely dressed, including coat, hat, and gloves, was all but frozen solid." The coroner cleared his throat. "I had to thaw him out before I could do the autopsy."

"Did he have any injuries?" Clayton asked.

"No obvious trauma."

The sheriff nodded. "So he died of exposure?"

"That's why you're the sheriff and I'm the coroner. No, he didn't die of exposure."

"Well, what the... Wait a minute," the sheriff barked. "I remember hearing about that. You ruined the day for a couple of detectives. And, if the rumors were true, you turned the case from damned odd to absolutely insane with your post mortem report. Didn't you claim the cause of death was drowning?"

"I didn't make any claims," the coroner said. "Just said it was so. He drowned."

"*Eewww,*" Abner Perry screeched. "No water in the car? No water in the building?"

The coroner shook his head. "Car was dry as a bone. Building had been turned off for decades."

"So you think he was... What?" Perry demanded. "Taken somewhere, drowned, then brought back and put in his car?" The lead paramedic shivered.

"Don't know," the coroner replied. "That's police business, not mine. Said it then, say it now; it's the gol-darnedest thing, but Soames drowned. And that wasn't all, not by a long shot." He passed a stare over the whole group. "You haven't heard the rest; nobody has."

"What... rest?" Henderson asked.

The coroner gave it some thought. "It's been a long while. *Ah*, hell. No one cares now anyhow." He nodded, giving himself permission to spill the beans. "When I got the lab reports back, toxicology and such, the story got even stranger. Soames drowned. But the water in his lungs was neither fluoridated nor chlorinated; it wasn't city water. Had microbes in it that suggested it had come from an untreated well. More than that, his lungs were a mess, residues of animal fat, sodium silicate, soda ash, several different pigments..." His voice trailed off. The Proprietor stared with a glint in his eye. The sheriff, firefighters, and medics stared blankly; several shrugged their ignorance. The coroner let the tension build. "Those are..." he finally said. "Strike that. Those *were* the chief ingredients of soap – as made by hand in the late 1800's."

The sound of the rain ruled the garage while the revelation sank in. Someone groaned. Several among the gathered laughed. Someone else, the coroner wasn't sure who, growled, "Oh, give me a break!"

"Believe it or don't," the coroner said. "That's your business, not mine. It wouldn't hurt though for some of you to be a tad more respectful. That's all any of us want, whether we're ghosts, or space aliens, or civil servants, or even just old county coroners... All we want, isn't it, a little respect?"

Sixteen

Though it clearly could have, it was not the horrendous smell alone that guided Herb Flay the last block to the scene of the removals. The neighborhood ahead was lit with blazing white flood lights from a fire engine, a ladder truck, an ambulance, two county squad cars, the sheriff's patrol car, and the coroner's station wagon, highlighted by the multiple red, blue, and yellow strobes from each, and fractured by the rain into glinting colored diamonds on the van's windshield. The gang was all there.

His boss, Marlowe Blake, was too.

Flay spotted the funeral home's gray boat of a Cadillac as he drew near, then saw Marlowe himself on the porch steps outside the house's wide-open front door. He was alone, of course. Flay spotted a couple of deputies in one of the county squads, a couple of firefighters in the cab of the fire engine, all wisely out of the rain. Where the sheriff, the coroner, and the rest of the rescuers were, Flay didn't know and didn't bother to guess. But leave it to funny ol' Marlowe to stand in the rain and that stink, pacing back and forth, grunting his anxiety to the heavens while he worried himself into a coma, convinced his assistant was never going to get there. Then Marlowe spotted the van, threw up his hands, and hurried down the drive to the street as quickly as his frame allowed.

Marlowe was built like a bundle of twigs with legs; short, guttish without being fat, thinning hair threatening to go gray, usually ginger in color but now darker, matted as it was to the top of his head by the rain, with nervous brown eyes and flailing hands (passed down from a Sicilian mother). He was in his late forties but, as has been mentioned before, he talked like an octogenarian climbing stairs, every fifth word or so prefaced with a breathy '*ehh*' to get him there.

Flay rolled down the van's window.

"I was afraid, *ehh*, you'd gotten lost."

"I had a flat tire, the–"

"*Ehh*, Herbert!" the funeral director interrupted, dripping rain water. "We'll talk, *ehh*, about it later." He pointed down the street, toward the Command Post garage, and told Flay that the coroner and company were waiting for them there. There, apparently, had to be some sort of meeting before the removals could be made.

"Did you want to–" Flay began, pointing to the passenger's seat.

"*Ehh*," Marlowe shouted in exasperation. "Go!"

Flay stepped on the gas, heading for the garage as instructed. Marlowe ran behind in the rain.

As Herb Flay pulled the funeral home van into the indicated driveway, the garage's overhead door started noisily up. To the young assistant, it looked like the curtain going up on a performance of *Le Théâtre du Grand-Guignol* – *the* wide door frame as proscenium arch, the garage as stage, and the cops, firefighters, medics, and one zealous neighbor inside as the players thereupon.

Marlowe, already well-informed about the situation, stood nervously by while the sheriff filled Flay in, with sweeping gestures at the horribly stinking house, on the items of information he needed to know. "There are two bodies inside – an elderly brother and sister. She's upstairs in a bedroom. He's below, in the garage under the house. The neighbor discovered them."

Flay followed the sheriff's gesture across the garage to where their host, despite the evening's events, was still beaming at and happily serving coffee to the emergency workers. *Why shouldn't the guy be having a good time*, Flay wondered. Why should he and Marlowe be the only ecstatic ones there?

"I hadn't seen the pair," the Proprietor said, "in... well... weeks really. Maybe a month." He laughed an odd laugh that wasn't really a laugh at all but, Flay imagined, just electric nerves. Then he went on with his story. "I went over to check on them. The bell didn't answer. So I made my way around the place and saw, well... I saw the insides of the windows covered with flies. Thousands, maybe tens of thousands, of flies inside the windows."

Flay took an offered cup of coffee from the excited neighbor. Marlowe passed.

The sheriff cleared his throat in a none-to-subtle attempt to drag the conversation back to the here and now. "The bodies," he said, "are–"

"They're deader than hell," the coroner put in bluntly.

Thunder boomed and lightning flashed as if in emphasis. It wasn't necessary, with the door wide open they could all smell that overriding fact.

But now the coroner appeared to have had more than enough of the night. He just wanted to get on and pushed the meeting to its conclusion. "Been dead for a long time, a month or more. Nothing I can do for 'em and I ain't going back in there. I'll come down to your place tomorrow, Marlowe, look 'em over, make out the paperwork. You take 'em there. No sense your place and mine smelling like this."

Marlowe smiled with lips pressed so tightly they nearly disappeared. The reason was no secret. The coroner's name was Art Grimsdyke. Outside of his county duties, he owned and operated the Arthur E. Grimsdyke Funeral Home on the opposite side of Sturm's Landing. Grimsdyke was Fengriffen's competition and, for the last few months, had gotten all of what little business the city presented. Now he was unashamedly handing the rotted ball off and graciously offering to stink up Fengriffen's embalming room to boot. Marlowe hated the coroner on a good day. And this wasn't turning into a good day.

A bit more talk followed, despite the coroner wanting to get on, to hold off the inevitable. But, finally, there was nothing left to do but commence the horror show, to enter the house and its pool of ungodly stink, and remove the bodies.

The uniforms were well-pleased Fengriffen's were there to handle that. The fire chief offered them the air packs, on display on the sawhorse table, if they wanted them. "They won't keep the smell out entirely," he admitted. "But the fresh air in your face will be a relief all the same."

Flay gladly accepted and, following a demonstration from Henderson that lasted all of two minutes, was clear enough on the basic operation to use the device without suffocating. Marlowe, in addition to his other quirks, was claustrophobic. For him, wearing the rubber mask would have been a nightmare on par with the work ahead of them and he passed on the offer. "*Ehh*, I'll, *ehh*, just hold my breath."

The van was returned half-way down the block and backed into the death house drive as near the front stoop as possible. The stretcher was rolled from the rear compartment and its legs dropped into place, and one of the rubber, zippered body bags was thrown on top of it. Flay twisted the valve on the air pack, secured the straps on the face mask and, with a slight blast of positive pressure, took in his first breath of freshly bottled air. It didn't kill the stink, of course, the fire chief had warned of that. Nothing could have, but it helped. Marlowe, without an air pack, took the deep breath he'd promised himself, pinched his lips to hold it against the awful stench, and led the stretcher and his re-hired assistant into the house through the front door. Throwing the rule book to the wind, on this one special occasion, the coroner, cops, and company waited outside in the rain.

Marlowe and Flay passed a dark and cluttered front room on the left, down a short hall, and entered a small, chaotic kitchen lit by a stark fluorescent ring above. Plastic flowers, oven mitts, a bunt cake pan, and a fish-shaped gelatin mold decorated the walls as in many an old lady's home. These differed in that they were flecked with bloated flies. The counter, the 'grandma' table, and the four chairs furnishing the room were barely visible beneath countless teetering stacks of books; these too were dotted liberally with buzzing flies. Hardcovers, soft covers, boxed sets, Trade paperbacks, paperbacks – romances, westerns, adventures and, as only seemed fitting, works of horror. That wasn't the end. There were easily as many non-fiction books (on seemingly any subject). It was a big world.

The brother and sister couple, it would later be revealed, had been librarians before they were corpses; both with a tendency to bring their work home. As he passed, Marlowe tapped a book atop one of the stacks. Dozens of flies took to the air buzzing madly. Flay grimaced, waved the darting insects from his mask with a blue rubber-gloved hand, and paused to examine the volume – a maroon hardcover, embossed with gold, entitled *Mortuary Science*. It was, apparently, also a small world.

Atop another stack of books lay a scattered handful of cream chocolates, several half-eaten. Around those and in a pile on the floor lay an eerie but impressive collection of dead flies.

The sister's corpse lay in her bed awash in her own putrescence. It was a scene reminiscent of the old Victorian photograph of Mary Jane Kelly following Jack the Ripper's final night of work. But the elderly spinster wasn't slashed. She'd been brutalized only by the poison that had killed her and, after death, by the ferocious forces of nature that return all once-sentient life forms to their origins. *Ashes to ashes. Dust to dust.* The lady had reached a gooey step in-between not mentioned in the text of the burial ceremony.

Marlowe caught sight of something man-made in the heart of the organic mess, leaned closer for a better look, and lifted a soaked piece of paper from her hand and the swamp that once had been her chest. A cloud of flies took to the air at the disturbance, hundreds, thousands; black chainsaws revving and flitting in circles. Marlowe, his mouth already clamped, now closed his eyes against the assault. Flay fogged his mask, breathing harder, as the little bastards bounced off his face piece. A moment – a long moment of disgust – and the living cloud began to settle. Marlowe held up the piece of paper, turned it dripping, for Flay to examine. It was a hand-written note, streaked and barely legible, confessing double suicide.

There was little point in waiting for the uproar of angry, frightened flies to end entirely as Flay and Marlowe's every movement sent a new wave of the revolting winged demons into the air. Agitated, fighting to keep his mouth closed and, it appeared, to hold in a scream welling in his chest, Marlowe pointed to the bed and the body. He wanted the deed done; the removal made. Flay was all for that.

There was no lifting her bodily as the lady was more soup than steak. Marlowe yanked the corners of the fitted sheet free on his side. Flay followed suit on his. They folded them in, wrapping the remains like Hell's burrito. Oddly, as they lifted dripping sheet-and-all into the body bag and Marlowe zipped it closed, Flay realized he was no longer hungry.

There's no need to repeat the narrative in reverse as, in a blizzard of darting flies, they retraced their steps backward, rolled her out through the front door, and lifted the now-occupied body bag into the van. They did – and were half-way home.

The other corpse was around back in the garage below. Flay followed orders and moved the van. Then he grabbed the second zippered bag and tossed it on the stretcher. Marlowe grabbed a deep and badly needed, if rain-filled, breath. One of the braver firefighters, Reid, who'd accompanied them, hit a switch and the garage door yawned open. A new wave of rot hit the night air like an escaping ghost.

As if the upstairs scene hadn't been creepy enough, the brother's corpse was sitting up-right in their old brown Buick. Really. The guy was buckled behind the steering wheel with lap and shoulder belts on as if he were headed out for a Sunday drive. *It was bizarre*, Flay thought, *and amusing in its own way.* Less comic was his condition. The old man's once pale skin was black and oozing with decay, his pastel blue shirt and trousers soaked dark in his own leaked fluids. A six-inch crucifix on a silver chain hung, inexplicably, about his neck and glistened on his chest in the beam of the firefighter's flashlight.

Marlowe pushed the stretcher to the side, laid the heavy bag on the floor, and unzipped and spread it wide. He studied the situation a moment, then led Flay back outside where the rain and cool air bathed them again, and the funeral director could grab another breath. Flay, in the air pack, couldn't feel his relief. On the other hand, Flay was avoiding the flies and the worst of the oppressive odor. "You undo, *ehh*, the seat belt," Marlowe told him, laying out his plan of attack. "I'll get the head and, *ehh*, shoulders first. Then you bring out, *ehh*, the feet."

The seat belt fought Flay, of course, but finally with a *click* released its hold on the occupant. He felt for Marlowe, having to push into the confined driver's space just below the headliner, to take the body under the arms, to feel the wispy hair of the rotted head against his cheek but, Flay also realized, the real terror was reserved for him. On his knees on the cold, oil-stained floor of the garage, between the door and the car's frame, beneath the steering column to grab the departed's ankles, he had no choice but to stare up into the face of the corpse. The eyes had rotted from its lolling head and, with the black lips and gums receded, it grinned down as if it knew a secret. More monster than man, it nodded forward as Marlowe tugged. Twitching maggots dropped from the hollow eye orbits and landed and stuck against his clear visor like rice pudding in a food fight. Flay screamed in the mask. Beyond his face piece, and the tiny writhing conqueror worms, the crucifix dangled in his face. With the rain falling outside the open door, with the lightning flashes, and the booming thunder, the icon offered no solace and only added to the horror.

Freed from the old Buick, the body was quickly deposited inside the rubber bag and zipped closed. The stretcher was hoisted and rolled out and, a moment later, brother and sister were reunited in the back of the funeral parlor's van. Flay closed the compartment doors, fell against them in relief, and pulled the air mask from his sweating head. The rain and cool night air slapped him like an open palm. The air remained rife with stink, the house remained full to the rafters with bloated flies; they would until the place was cleaned or leveled, but the source had been bottled.

Speaking of bottles... Flay returned his air pack to Paul Henderson at the ladder truck.

The Command Post was being broken down.

The ambulance had been sent as an automatic precaution when the bodies had first been discovered. Now that they'd been removed, and all of the responding civil servants were out of danger, the reason for the ambulance no longer existed. The ambulance crew bid their goodbyes and pulled away, headed for their home garage on the outskirts of Sturm's Landing; the excited Clayton driving, with the events of a night to remember (and a new war story of her very own) turning in her head, the revolted Perry with nothing in his head but the remnants of a night to forget.

There was some witty banter among the remaining emergency workers, inappropriate jokes to erase what remained of the tension as they secured their vehicles. The mortician's assistant thought of a few, but the *respectful propriety* of his position prevented Flay from joining in. Henderson stored the air bottle Flay had emptied, put the air pack harnesses away, stashed the heavy duty 'key' with which he and the deputies had knocked in the front door lock, and made ready to hit the road. Henderson pulled the ladder truck out and roared away. With the fire chief in his command seat, and Reid and Baker in their jump seats behind, Lund shut down the engine's flashing 'emergency' light bar, put the engine in gear, and vanished with her Company into the dark.

Fengriffen's van was loaded and Flay was ready to go. With an "*Ehh*. Herbert, thank you. I'll, *ehh*, see you back at the funeral home," from funny ol' Marlowe, the mortician's assistant was on his way.

The sheriff and his deputies sealed up the fly-filled house. They debated whether or not to break out the *Crime Scene* tape but, in the end, decided against it. They had their suicide note. Besides, there was obviously no extended family interested enough to raise a stink or demand further investigation.

"What did you say the neighbor's name was?" the sheriff asked Maitland, the pair of them hurrying through the rain to thank the gentleman for his assistance.

"My notebook is in the squad," the deputy said. "It's Schreck or Shanks; something like that."

The sheriff frowned and entered the garage, leaving Maitland out in the rain. He thanked the Proprietor for his help and generosity, shook his hand heartily, and didn't even make a face at the fishy handshake he got in return. "What was the name again?" the sheriff asked.

"Smith," the Proprietor said with a grin. "Just Smith."

The lights of Cedartown became pinpoints again, then faded altogether as the village disappeared into the night behind Fengriffen's van and Herb Flay. It was still raining, but the thunder had ended and the lightning had calmed to a distant infrequent flicker. The special effects were ending and the horror show, it appeared, was finally over. And that house had been a horror show. So much different than it had looked before.

Yes, Herb Flay had been there before.

He'd met the couple, more than four months earlier, when he first came to town. Flay was a big reader, always had been. And, when one was looking for work in a new town, the library was a good place to start. Funerals had been his stock in trade; funeral homes his comfort zone. But one didn't just pop into a mortuary and fill out an application. One had to learn the local history, the background, the management. Jim and Emily Underwood, the names of his cargo, the brother and sister couple bagged-up in the back of the van, had been a great help in his researches. With their assistance, he learned all he needed to know about funny ol' Marlowe and the Henry Fengriffen Funeral Home. Thanks to them and, of course, thanks to his own personal charms, securing a position had been a walk in the park.

Later, the Underwoods had been there to help all over again, without even knowing it. They'd been so open; told him all he needed to know about themselves. They were a desperately lonely couple, no other family, few friends, just the library and each other. And they had burial prearrangements already made with the Fengriffen Funeral Home. The perfect people to know. When the bottom fell out of the 'dying' business, and Flay needed a body and a funeral to save his job, they were right there in reserve, ready to provide one. Two, actually. They never suspected.

The neighbors, including the nosy Mr. Smith, hadn't taken the least notice. They couldn't have cared less. And the Underwoods had grown so fond of him, it was perfectly natural for Flay to drop by their house. He'd helped Jim carry in books. He'd gobbled several of Emily's homemade muffins. He'd returned that copy of *Mortuary Science* he'd borrowed and, as a way of saying 'Thank you', had brought a big box of chocolates. They'd both confessed to having a sweet tooth, hadn't they?

It was no trouble at all to return the following night, to park a block away, to slip through a window he'd left unfastened. What he'd found on his second visit had been – strange. They'd eaten the laced candy and both of the Underwoods were dead, of course. Emily, in her bed; normal for someone with a tummy ache. But Jim. . . Flay had a few terror stricken minutes while he searched for the old boy. And breathed a huge sigh of relief when he found him. Just what the heck Jim was doing in his car, down in the basement garage, Heaven only knew. They had no telephone. Why should they? Who would those two sad sacks call? Perhaps when Jim felt the churning, he got it in his mind to go for help? Who knew for sure? Flay wasn't Sherlock Holmes and it didn't make any difference. He found Jim, as dead as his sister, and that's all that was needed. He dumped the remaining candy on the piled books on the kitchen table and took the box away. He scribbled a suicide note (with neither excess dramatics nor a wordy explanation) and put it in Emily's hand on her chest. He slipped back out, unseen, into the dark.

That was a month ago.

Flay had no idea it would end in a lesson. In business, as in comedy, timing was everything. It had taken too long for the bodies to be discovered. Had it not been for the flies and the nosy neighbor, Flay would have lost his job, his efforts would have gone for nothing, and the Underwoods would have gone to waste. There were benefits to helping the lonely to their final reward. They weren't quickly missed and you had time to get away. But, now he realized, if the chosen were too lonely and forgotten, they might not be found at all. What good was that? There's no point removing someone if, when the time comes, you're no longer employed to do the removal. He would need to plan more carefully the next time business slowed.

Speaking of slow. . . The rain had eased to a drizzle by the time he reached the city and stopped entirely as the lights of the funeral home appeared ahead. The morning air was fresh as lemons and, hot dog, his sinus passages were starting to clear.

Come to think of it, Herb Flay was hungry again.

About the Author

Doug Lamoreux is a father of three, a grandfather, a writer, and actor. A former professional firefighter, he is the author of seven novels, a novella, and a contributor to anthologies and non-fiction works including the Rondo Award nominated Horror 101, and its companion, the Rondo Award winning Hidden Horror. He has been nominated for a Rondo, a Lord Ruthven Award, a Pushcart Prize, and is the first-ever recipient of The Horror Society's Igor Award for fiction. Lamoreux starred in the 2006 Peter O'Keefe film, Infidel, and appeared in the Mark Anthony Vadik horror films The Thirsting (aka Lilith) and Hag.

Other books by Doug Lamoreux:

- The Devil's Bed
- Dracula's Demeter
- The Melting Dead
- Corpses Say the Darndest Things: A Nod Blake Mystery
- When the Tik-Tik Sings

Other books by Doug Lamoreux and Daniel D. Lamoreux:

- Apparition Lake
- Obsidian Tears

CPSIA information can be obtained
at www.ICGtesting.com
Printed in the USA
BVHW091759280121
599006BV00037B/4131/J

9 781034 171973